MUSINGS FROM A DEMENTED MIND

BY

DEREK AILES & JAMES COOM

*To Mari
Stay Scared
Dennis*

This is a work of fiction. The events and characters described herein are imaginary and are not intended to refer to specific places or living persons. The opinions expressed in this manuscript are solely the opinions of the author and do not represent the opinions or thoughts of the publisher. The author has represented and warranted full ownership and/or legal right to publish all the materials in this book.

Musings From A Demented Mind
All Rights Reserved
Copyright 2015 Derek Ailes

This book may not be reproduced, transmitted, or stored in whole or in part by any means, including graphic, electronic, or mechanical without the express written consent of the publisher except in the case of brief quotations embodied in critical articles and reviews.
Weekland Press
Printed in the United States of America

For information and permission request contact: derekailes2003@comcast.net
Published in the United States by Weekland Press.

Website: http://www.derekailes.com

Also Available:

Zombie Command: A Horror Anthology

Beast Within: Coming in 2016

With Author Mark Cusco Ailes:

Journey Into the Unknown: Deluxe Horror Edition

Catfurnado, Zombies and One Killer Doll

Dedicated to the memory of James Coon
(July 5, 1952 – March 28, 2015)

Musings From J.C.'s Mind

Yes, Mother!

Willis sat at his desk looking at the photo album filled with pictures of his mother who had passed away several days before. He finally, after several days of dealing with contacting all his relatives, planning the funeral, and burying her body, had a chance to think about how his life would be without her. He was fifty-two years old and for the first time in his life, he would have to live alone in his mother's house. He had lived with his mother for the past twenty years. He had an ex-wife and two kids living in Nevada he hadn't seen since the divorce, but kept in contact with them through Facebook and Skype. He stared at the stacks of comic books sitting by his bed. Behind them were several stacks of paperback books ranging from horror and science fiction to nonfiction dealing with alien abductions and haunted houses and graveyards. Next to those were years' worth of magazines dealing with the unexplained and ghostly encounters.

"Clean up this mess. You're in your fifties. This isn't a junk yard," he could still hear his mother complain.

"Yes, mother," Willis responded like he did every time. This time there wasn't anyone there to respond.

He stared at the picture of his parents on their wedding day. He tried to hold back his tears realizing both of his parents were now reunited in the afterlife. The only family who lived close by was his sister, Gabby, who he barely spoke to. He turned to the page where his high school graduation pictures with his mother were. He was handsome back then with a clean shaven face and thin glasses. Now he had a large, unkempt, greying beard with thick glasses. He looked like he was a family member of the Duck Dynasty.

"You should shave! You're not a hobo!"

"Yes, mother!"

He looked toward the hallway expecting to see her staring at him, but there was nothing. All he could see was the large bookcase filled with all of her favorite romance novels. His sister wanted to take the books away, but he wouldn't have it. All of his mother's possessions were precious and there was no way anyone was going to take them away from the house. Those items were his mom's treasures which made them his treasures.

He closed the photo album and placed it to the left of his computer. He opened the writing program on the computer and worked on his science fiction novel he had been working on for several years. He wanted to finish it and get it published, but he could never keep his mind focused long enough to write more than a couple of pages a day.

"Willis, are you on the computer again? Being naughty aren't you? You should get a girlfriend! That's what a normal person would do!"

"Yes, mother!"

He looked at the bookcase again wondering why he was hearing her voice when she no longer was there. He tried writing some more of his novel, but he couldn't get the voice of his mother out of his head. He slowly stood up and walked out of his bedroom toward the kitchen. He grabbed a potato off of the kitchen table, which was filled with cans of food he had bought at the dollar store the other day, and put it in the microwave. As he waited for it to cook, he read the morning's newspaper. As he heard the beeping from the microwave, he put the paper down.

"Put the paper in the recycling bin when you're done!"

"Yes, mother!"

After eating the potato, he walked back into his bedroom and grabbed a paperback off the stack of books he hadn't read yet. He read several chapters and put the book down as he heard someone pounding on his wall. He slowly got up and walked into the living room, but no one was there. He heard the pounding coming from his bedroom and when he walked into it no one was there. He could hear the pounding again coming from the living room, but no one was there.

"Who is knocking on the walls?"

No one answered.

He sat down on his chair in the living room and turned on the television. He watched the news station until he dozed off. When he awoke, he could see sunlight through the faded blue curtains. He had slept the whole night through on his chair. He slowly pulled himself out of the chair and walked toward the bathroom. All the romance novels were scattered on the floor in front of the bookcase. He kneeled down and placed them neatly back onto the bookcase. All of his other stacks of books in his bedroom were still standing. He stared at the bookcase trying to figure out how those books fell off it.

He slowly walked up the stairs leading to his mother's bedroom. On her bed was one of her romance books with her favorite bookmark of a cat hanging from a rope. He looked in shock since there wasn't anything on her bed the day before.

"Mother?" he said, slowly stuttering.

No answer.

He walked out of her bedroom and into the bathroom hoping a soothing bath would clear his head. He tried to reassure himself he was imagining things and the book had been on the bed, and he just hadn't noticed it before.

"Make sure you clean the soap scum out of the tub when you're done!"

"Yes, mother!"

After his bath, he scrubbed the tub and walked into his bedroom. He got on the internet and checked his Facebook page. It was filled with condolences from some of his friends who had recently learned of his mother's passing. He checked on the statuses of his children and then went on a website dealing with hauntings of loved ones. According to the website, it was common for loved one's spirits to linger around their homes after death, but only a few people possessed the ESP ability to sense their presence. He always felt a strange presence when he visited someone's house like there was someone else there besides those he could see. It was worse when he visited cemeteries. He always sensed there was something paranormal haunting them which was one of the reasons why he became obsessed with books about ghosts and haunted houses.

He was startled by the sound of someone knocking on the front door. He slowly pulled himself out of the chair and walked into the living room. He looked out the window and saw his sister standing on the porch. He stood there debating if he should answer the door for fear she was going to try to take some of his mother's belongings.

"She's your sister! Answer the door!"

"Yes, mother!" he said as he opened the door.

His sister stared at him for a few seconds and spoke, "I thought you were going to leave me standing out here all day."

"I thought about it. What do you want?"

"I was in the neighborhood, and I stopped by to check on you."

"I'm fine."

"Can I come in?"

He turned around.

"Is there someone in here with you?"

He turned back around. "No, why do you ask?"

"It looked like you were waiting for someone to give you permission."

"Sorry, habit. I'm used to making sure mother was decent for company. Come in." He walked over to his chair and sat down.

"I met with our lawyer about mom's will. As we all expected, she left you the house. She left me all of her collectibles in the display cases."

"Gabby, those are mom's collectibles," he said in shock. "They belong in her house."

"I want them. You get everything else in the house. I want those. I want something to remember her by."

"No, you're probably going to sell them for money!" He quickly jumped out of his chair like he had the strength from when he was in his teens. Gabby sat back in fear. His hands were shaking like he could attack her in his present mindset.

"I don't need any money. Mom left both of us plenty of money. See for yourself." She handed him a copy of their mother's will. "She took care of us."

"Sorry. I didn't mean to scare you," he said, regaining his composure. "I'm just afraid if her things leave this house, I'll begin to forget her." He put his hands over his face trying to stop himself from crying. "Just take them now."

"I brought some egg boxes from the grocery store. I'll go get them." Gabby walked out of the house to her car.

"You made the right decision."

"Yes, mother," he said softly, staring at the display cases.

Several hours after Gabby left with all the collectibles from the display cases, Willis sat at the kitchen table eating a bowl of beef stew and listening to a soundtrack score to one of his favorite horror movies. Once he was finished eating, he walked to his bedroom to read until it was time to go to bed. As he was dozing off, he placed the book on his nightstand and turned off the light. As he was sleeping, he began to feel like something heavy was pushing down on his chest. He snapped awake. Above him was a large, black apparition with glowing red eyes. He tried to move, but he was paralyzed. The paralysis was not from fear. He was not frightened by the apparition. Something was keeping him from moving, as if an invisible force was holding him down. Even in the darkness, he recognized the apparition's face. It was the face of his mother. The apparition stared down at him for several minutes before vanishing. As it vanished, he could feel the pressure lessening on his body. He slowly crawled out of bed and turned on the light. He grabbed the towel he kept by the side of the bed just in case he got sick and couldn't make it to the bathroom at night, and wiped the sweat off his forehead. He knew he hadn't dreamed about the apparition. It was real.

He sat down in front of his computer. He felt all of his sadness leave his body, replaced with a sense of happiness knowing he was being haunted, not by some evil spirit, but by his mother. He sat down and for two days straight he wrote, only stopping to eat and go to the bathroom, and continued writing his science fiction novel until it was finally completed. Once he was satisfied the book was the best he could write it, he wrote one final sentence. I dedicate this novel to my loving mother. I know she will be with me always. I will never forget her.

With his dedication finished, he emailed his novel to his friend who worked at a publishing company and who had promised his novel would make it to print once he finally completed it. He lay down on his bed and closed his eyes. A couple of hours later he felt a sharp pain in his chest and when he opened his eyes, his mother was standing next to his bed all dressed in white with a bright light behind her.

"Willis, it is time to take you home," she said with a smile and helped him out of the bed.

With his hand in her's, he said, "yes, mother," and followed her into the light.

Golden Age Retirement and Rehabilitation Center

Evan stared at the tiny television screen attached to the wall across from him at the Golden Age Retirement and Rehabilitation Center, watching the William Shatner episode of the Twilight Zone where the creature was on the wing of the plane. Four weeks prior, he had his left leg amputated a few inches below his knee. His doctor warned him if he didn't have the amputation, he would be dead within the month. He was staying in the rehabilitation wing of the retirement home waiting for his leg to heal so his doctor could fit him for an artificial leg. The only thing he felt like doing besides watching television was reading several murder mysteries.

He looked toward the window trying to see if the sun was shining, but the only thing he could see was the damn concrete fountain outside. He wanted to go outside and breathe some fresh air and go to the store and gets some real snacks. The type that would cause his sugar to spike high. He was diabetic and the diabetes was out of control. He took multiple pills to keep his sugar lowered. *Hell, his whole tote bag was one giant medicine cabinet.* He had a taste for some lemon ice tea and a candy bar. Maybe some microwave popcorn would do the trick. The snacks he was provided there were as tasteless as cardboard. Plain rice cakes probably tasted better.

He heard a rasping noise from the bed adjacent to his. Melvin, who recently suffered a stroke, was gasping for air. Evan pressed the call button for the nurse and a minute later Breanne, the heavyset African American nurse, walked in. He pointed over at the other bed and the nurse, hearing him gasping, rushed over to him. She quickly ran out of the room and a few seconds later, two other nurses along with one of the doctors ran in.

"I think he's having another stroke," Evan said as she pulled his curtain around blocking his view of them working on Melvin.

After a few minutes, he heard the doctor say he was stabilized. He felt a sigh of relief. The last thing he wanted was to stay in the same room where another patient had died. He recalled the night when he felt chest pains and managed to drive himself to the hospital. It was there his doctor decided he needed the amputation done urgently.

The nurse pulled his curtain back.

"He's ok."

"I knew something didn't sound right."

"I'm glad you paged me or he may have died," Breanne said. "Now I think it's time for you to take your meds."

"You might as well bring me a gallon of water to wash them down."

"It's not that many."

"Then why do I tell the pharmacist to give me one of everything each time I go Walgreens?"

"It's good to have a sense of humor. It helps with the recovery." With a smile, she handed him a cup with all his medications.

"Bottoms up," he said and began to swallow each of the pills followed by plenty of water. "Do I need to lift my tongue up and prove I swallowed them?"

"This isn't a psych ward."

"Can you bring me some microwave popcorn?" he asked as she was walking out of the room. "I guess that would be a no."

The next couple of hours were uneventful and he felt really bored. After eating dinner, he slid off the bed into his wheelchair and wandered into the hallway. He saw Kenner, another patient, sitting outside his room having a conversation with himself about the Vietnam War and how he avoided being drafted.

"Kenner, Vietnam ended decades ago."

"What!"

Evan shook his head as he wheeled past him. He passed the dining area and headed for the Pepsi machine past the kitchen. He put a dollar in and pressed the button for a Pepsi. He looked around making sure no nurses were around to witness him drinking a sugary soda. As he was about to finish the soda, he heard a buzzing noise coming from the back hallway where his room was located. He threw the can into the garbage and quickly pushed his wheelchair forward to see what was happening. As he rounded the corner, he saw a nurse bringing Kenner back in through the glass door at the end of the hallway.

"Who forgot to lock the door?" the head nurse asked angrily.

"I must have," Shelly, the short and petite brunette nurse who Evan had passionate dreams about each night, said. "I went out for a smoke and apparently forgot to lock it."

"Shelly, I can't allow this to go unpunished. You are suspended for a week. From now on, nobody uses this door for any reason. It will remain locked."

Shelly tried to hide her face as she passed by Evan. He stared at her cute, tight behind as she disappeared down the hallway.

"Great, one less thing to look at for a week."

He wheeled himself back toward his room.

"I almost got away," Kenner laughed as a nurse pushed him past Evan.

"Almost." Evan said as he returned to his room to read another book.

The next morning, Breanne brought him a plate of turkey and mashed potatoes. He lifted up his plate and, trying to sound like Oliver Twist, said "Please sir, I want some more."

With a laugh she said. "You try that bit on me every morning."

"I could really use some more potatoes."

"That's one serving exactly. Remember, your strict diet."

"My pills are more filling than this."

"And less calories," she said as she left.

He looked over at the daily newspaper and thought about adding some fiber to his meal. He looked up at the television and the channel was still in the middle of a Twilight Zone marathon. They were showing the episode where Roddy McDowall crash lands on Mars, which was one of his favorites.

After watching several more episodes, he climbed into his wheelchair and went for a stroll of the facility. Kenner was down the hall having a conversation with the Invisible Man or a ghost possibly. As he got closer, he could hear him talk about some secret experiment going on over at the retirement wing of the building. Kenner nodded repeatedly as if someone was talking back. Evan shook his head as he wheeled past him.

In the dining area, a priest was leading the morning sermon to a group of the elderly residents of the retirement wing. He stopped and listened and after the closing prayer, he continued on with the stroll. Every doctor and nurse said hello to him as they passed. Once he was to the front, he asked if he could go outside. As one of the nurses pressed the button, the automatic doors opened outward and he rolled outside. The nurse followed him outside and walked to the end of the sidewalk to have a smoke. The sky was cloudy and it looked like a thunderstorm was on the way. There was a refreshing chill to the air and he was happy to be outside enjoying it. He had been experiencing cabin fever and the chill was somewhat of a temporary cure.

He looked over at the long brick wall of the retirement wing and wondered if Kenner was telling the truth about secret experiments going on over there. And if there were, who were the test subjects? There were a lot of residents who had Alzheimer's. Maybe they were trying to come up with a cure.

He was the opposite. He possessed an eidetic memory. People were astonished at how he could remember everything anybody ever told him down to the exact word. Some of his co-workers claimed he missed his calling as a blackmailer. What they didn't know was he could also read lips. Because of his speech and hearing impairment as a child, he went to a special school to learn sign language and read lips. Over the years, thanks to watching television religiously and going to the theater with his father, he learned to speak properly. He was well read and, thanks to his eidetic memory, he remembered everything he ever read from his favorite childhood book "Charlotte's Web" to thousands of mystery and science fiction novels he read ever since.

"Are you ready to go back in or can I smoke another cigarette?" Christine asked.

"You can smoke the whole pack if you want."

"Don't tempt me," she joked as she lit another one up.

He watched her walk away. Her shiny, raven black hair flowed in the wind. She had black framed glasses that gave her extra sex appeal to a nerd like him. She was a short, beautiful Hispanic woman in her early twenties. If it wasn't for her constant smoking, she would be perfect. Having a sense a humor was also a plus.

As lightning began, she informed him it was time to go back in. She wheeled him back inside as the rain poured down. A few minutes later, the tornado sirens went off outside.

"All staff and patients, a tornado has been spotted in our area. Move everybody to the designated tornado areas," the head nurse announced over the PA system.

"Finally, some excitement," Evan laughed as he followed Christine over to the dining area.

The staff moved all the patients in wheelchairs to the dining area within seconds. The ones who were bedridden, their beds were rolled to the hallway past the dining room where there were no windows.

As the power went out and the emergency lights instantly came on, Evan noticed that a few of the older residents were unaccounted for.

"Christine, where's Janine and Julie?"

"They both passed away last night," she answered sadly.

"Oh, I'm sorry to hear that."

"They were both good people. They died peacefully."

As the severe storm passed, everybody was allowed to go back to their rooms. As Evan was heading back to his room, he was stopped by Kenner.

"Evan, do you want to know a secret?" He looked to the right of him and spoke to the invisible person next to him. "Yes, we can trust him."

"What's the secret?"

"Janine and Julie are alive. They took them to experiment on."

"Who took them?"

Kenner looked around afraid they were being watched. He leaned closer and whispered, "the government."

"I think your imagination is running wild. Christine said they died and I'll believe her before I believe you."

"Fine. When they come for you, don't say I didn't try to warn you," Kenner said and wheeled himself into his room.

"And people say I'm the crazy one."

The next morning, Evan's doctor, Neal Eckes, examined his leg. "It is healing very nicely."

"How long until I can get my prosthesis?"

"I will re-examine your leg in two weeks and then I'll make my decision."

"Ok."

"Keep a positive attitude."

"I always do, Doctor."

A short, beautiful nurse with long curly hair walked into his room followed by Breanne. She possessed a striking resemblance to Taylor Swift.

"Hello," Evan greeted her excitedly.

"This is Jenna. She's a new trainee fresh out of nursing school."

"A new victim."

"Down, Evan. She's young enough to be your granddaughter."

"I'm not that old," Evan laughed.

"Who was president when you were born?"

"Truman."

"I think I made my point." She looked over at Jenna. "Watch this one. He's trouble."

"I think I can handle him."

Another beautiful nurse with long, strawberry-blonde hair and freckles all over her face and arms walked in.

"Breanne, I finished giving Walter his shots," she informed her.

"Evan, stop drooling," Breanne laughed as she handed him a Kleenex. "This is Juliana. This is also her first day."

"Hello, Evan."

"You know my name already. I'm not sure that is a good thing."

"Mental note to self, he's a flirt. Don't worry. I'm a flirt too," she teased.

"I like her," he said to Breanne.

"I figured you would. We better leave before we give Evan a heart attack," Breanne joked and led them out of the room.

"Bye girls." He waived at them as they left. "This is such an amazing place for a bachelor."

He slid himself into his wheelchair and left his room in hopes of seeing one of the new nurses bending over to pick something up. Across from his room, Kenner sat staring at Juliana suspiciously. Evan wheeled himself over to him.

"Kenner, is there something wrong?"

"I've seen pictures of Julie when she was a teenager. The nurse could be her twin."

"What are you implying?"

"Think about it. Julie. Juliana."

"Your point?"

"Maybe the experiments are to make them young again."

"Are you implying there are alien cocoons in the swimming pool outside?"

"Huh?"

Kenner looked at him confused. It was apparent he had never seen the movie "Cocoon".

"Just an old movie reference."

"Movies? I remember seeing movies in Chesterton where the Ben Franklin used to be for a quarter. Now the kids are paying a buck or two."

"It hasn't been that cheap in decades."

"What are you talking about? I just saw 'Raiders of the Lost Ark' the other day at the General Cinema for a buck."

"The General Cinema was torn down decades ago."

"What year is it?"

"2015."

"I think he lost his marbles. He thinks it's the future," Kenner laughed, looking over to his imaginary friend. He began to have a long conversation with him.

Evan took this as an opportunity to wheel himself away unnoticed. He continued down the hallway and saw Julianna talking with Jenna. They stopped talking when they spotted him.

"Ladies," he said as he passed by them.

Once he was out of hearing range, they continued their conversation.

He made it to the dining area and stared at the retirement wing for several minutes recalling the conversation he had with Kenner. He wheeled forward toward the retirement wing and was stopped by a tall black doctor wearing a long white uniform reminding him of an orderly in a mental institution.

"Sir, you can't pass beyond this point. The retirement wing is currently off limits," he instructed.

"Why?"

"There's an illness going around. It's on quarantine. Don't worry. It's not fatal, but it is nasty."

Evan try to see past him, but the doorway was closed.

"Sir, can you please go back the way you came."

"I will. I just got bored and wanted to do some exploring."

"I can have a nurse paged to take you back to your room."

"That is ok. I know the way."

He turned his wheelchair around and headed back to his room certain that Kenner was right about something suspicious going on in the retirement wing. His curiosity was getting the best of him, and he changed direction toward the front door. *Christine's shift started a couple hours ago and she may want to go outside and smoke. While she is preoccupied with her cigarette, I can wheel myself over to the windows of the retirement wing and see if I can get a glimpse of what is going on inside.*

"Christine, interested in a smoke?"

She looked up from her desk and smiled at him. She stood up, grabbed a pack of cigarettes from her purse, and walked up to the front door unlocking it. She pushed him through to the outside and then walked to the end of the sidewalk to smoke. As she was smoking and checking her messages on her smartphone, he wheeled across the sidewalk toward one of the glass windows of the retirement wing. He glanced behind him making sure she wasn't paying any attention to him and stopped at the window and looked inside. He saw a couple of beautiful young women walking down the hallway. He watched impatiently for a few minutes hoping to see anything suspicious.

As he was about to glance back to see where Christine was, he felt a large hand grab his shoulder. Before he could react, a man forcefully placed a towel over his face. Within seconds, he lost consciousness.

As his eyes opened, he saw the black doctor from the hallway standing above him. He was strapped to a gurney and the doctor was staring at him smiling. He looked over to the right of him and saw a large, moss covered brown sphere.

"Are you going to make me younger like in the movie 'Cocoon'?"

"Not the movie title I would use."

Something was pushing through the sphere and, like an egg, it cracked as something began to climb out of it. It looked like an overgrown albino spider with a long tail. It reminded him of the face hugger from the movie "Alien". It looked over at him for a few seconds and jumped several feet in the air landing on his face. The last thing he remembered was the creature burrowing its way down his throat.

Kenner watched the television in the recreation room. His wife had brought him a stack of DVDs she found at the Goodwill down the street. One of them was his favorite movie "Invasion of the Body Snatchers".

"Kenner's in here," Breanne shouted.

Jenna and Juliana walked into the room followed by a new doctor Kenner had never seen before. His heart started beating faster as he realized the new doctor looked like Evan, but forty some years younger.

"Hello, Kenner. I'm Dr. Edward Koontz. According to your chart, you suffer from dementia." He looked over at the two nurses. "He'll make a perfect candidate. Take him to the retirement wing."

"Yes, doctor," the two nurses said, smiling.

Sirens of Lake Station

"Thank you for an enjoyable evening."

"My name is Jake," I answered as both of us were standing in my hotel room.

"Mine is Vicki," she said as she put her grey t-shirt with the word PINK written across it back on. "Are you sure you can't stay longer?"

"No, I've got a sales meeting in South Bend in a few hours. I guess this is goodbye."

She looked at me sadly as she brushed her straight, black hair with a pink hairbrush. With a sinister laugh, she said, "We'll be meeting a lot sooner than you can possibly believe."

She walked over to me and gave me a kiss on my left cheek. My heart was telling me to stay, but I knew I had to be at the sales meeting. If I didn't land the deal, I was going to be fired. My boss promised me that. She continued laughing sinisterly as she walked out the door.

As the closing door echoed through the room, I said, "That is what I get for picking up a hitchhiker."

I headed for the bathroom to take a shower and shave. After a twenty minute shower, I headed back into the bedroom to change into my grey business suit. I opened up my briefcase and checked to see if I remembered to put my new business cards in. I walked over to the window and saw the hood of my midnight blue Dodge Neon sticking straight up. I grabbed my briefcase and ran out of the room and over to my car. Being someone who knows nothing about mechanics, I did not know if somebody had tampered with it. I closed the hood and checked to make sure nobody slashed my tires. Satisfied nothing appeared to be wrong, I got into the car and felt a sigh of relief as the car started right up.

I drove out of the parking lot and headed for the exit leading to the interstate. Five minutes down the road, I began to hear a sound coming from under the hood like metal grinding on metal. The check engine light came on. I cursed and turned right at the next intersection. I could see a sign up ahead that said: Welcome to Lake Station. To the left of the sign was a gas station with a repair shop. I pulled into the parking lot just as the car stalled. I turned the key and it wouldn't start. I got out of the car as a mechanic walked over to me.

"Someone has been playing with my engine."

"Open the hood and I'll see what's wrong."

I popped open the hood and the mechanic did an inspection. "Someone did a beautiful job on your engine, mister," he said sarcastically.

"Can it be fixed in two hours?"

"I'll be lucky to have it done today."

"Damn, I've got to be in South Bend in a few hours. Can I use your phone?"

"Our cell phone service isn't working at the moment. Something's blocking the signal. Probably one of those solar flares I keep hearing about on the news. You can check the Walgreens across the street. They have a landline. I'll get to work on your car right away."

"Thanks," I said as I handed him the keys. "I'll be right back."

I walked over to Walgreens and walked in. I didn't see any sales clerks at the front counter so I headed toward the pharmacy in the back. I walked past the magazine aisle when I heard a loud alarm going off from outside. It sounded similar to the sirens I hear going off constantly during severe thunderstorms. When I walked into the store, there wasn't a cloud in the sky. As I was heading back to the front door to see what was going on, somebody grabbed my arm.

"If you go outside, you will die."

The badge on his uniform stated he was the store manager.

"What are you talking about?"

"They're going to get you?"

"Who are they?"

"The sirens."

"What is a siren?"

"They bestow the kiss of death."

He grabbed my arm and forced me through the swinging doors leading to the backroom.

"What the hell is going on?" I asked angrily.

"In the middle of Main Street is a gateway leading to death."

"Death?" I asked giving him a suspicious look.

"They sing to put you in a trance. Once they have you in their power, they will kiss you and drain the life force completely from your body."

"What the hell are you talking about? This is complete nonsense." By this point, I was getting annoyed by his paranoia.

"On Main Street there is a hidden gateway mankind can't see. It is where they come from."

All of a sudden, I heard a faint singing voice from the distance.

"They come through the gateway so they can claim victims to satisfy their lust," he continued.

"This is the real world. Mythical creatures don't exist," I argued.

"You don't know about the history of Lake Station. They've demanded a human sacrifice for one of them each year for centuries. Today is the day."

"You've got to be kidding me! Are the people in this town so primitive they would let human life go like cattle?"

"We have to. Their singing makes us."

Our conversation was interrupted by someone screaming, "Help!"

The singing was getting louder as if it was coming directly from outside the swinging metal doors.

"Jack, Jeff is acting funny! He's under the sirens' spell!"

The store manager rushed out the back room and ran to Jeff who was standing with a blank expression on his face as he was being beckoned by the song of the sirens. He grabbed Jeff's shoulders and shook him violently. "Why didn't you have sex last night?"

"I...couldn't...find...my...wife...last...night," Jeff slowly said as he was still under the spell.

Jeff's body became stiff and it rose several feet off of the floor. The store manager grabbed onto his legs and held onto him tightly.

"Let me go! I have to have her! She belongs to me and I belong to her! My dream! My Love! My Life!" Jeff screamed.

"Mister, please help me," the store manager pleaded as I rushed over to them.

I grabbed onto Jeff's arm and held it tightly. The singing was getting louder as if it was coming closer and closer. Jeff jerked violently forward causing both the store manager and me to fall backward from the force. Jeff slowly landed on the floor. A few seconds later a tall, beautiful woman with silver hair and glowing red eyes appeared. Her skin was silver and she was wearing a silver dress that was a shade darker than her skin. Her hair stood straight up like it was full of a strong electrical charge. She slowly walked over to Jeff and put her right hand seductively on his chest. She was singing while her mouth moved seductively with every word. She cocked her head to the side and raised her hands. Jeff's body rose several feet in the air and then she floated upward until her head was aligned with his.

"You're all mine. My love. My Life," Jeff chanted repeatedly.

She began to kiss his lips. As she continued to kiss him, his body caved in as she sucked his insides out through his mouth. As his whole body became flat as a sheet of plywood, he fell to the ground. The siren stared at us for a few seconds and walked away.

I couldn't move at all being frozen in fear.

"Is everybody ok?" the store manager asked a few seconds later. He kneeled down over what was left of Jeff and prayed. He looked up toward me.

"For the rest of my life, I will never forget what I witnessed here." I said.

"I've witnessed this happen several times in my lifetime."

"Why don't you people move? Just pack up and leave?"

"I don't know. It has never occurred to me to leave. Why?" he asked confused.

"You people are crazy! Why was he so attracted to her, but not the rest of us?"

"They only claim men who will give in to their sexual advances. I wasn't affected because my wife and I had sex last night. You have to have sex the night before or they will be able to claim you. Did you have sex last night?"

"I picked up a female hitchhiker last night. She spent the night with me at my hotel."

"You're a very lucky man, my friend."

I looked at him confused. I asked him again why the people of the town didn't leave.

"I'm not sure. I just have this desire to stay here for the rest of my life."

I looked down at what was left of Jeff and decided it was time to get out of Lake Station for good. I walked away from him. As I walked around the corner, someone grabbed my arm. I turned around and Vicki was standing before me.

"I told you we'd be seeing each other again," she said seductively.

"It was you. You were the one who tampered with my car." I looked at her angrily.

She rubbed her right hand across my chest and laughed playfully. "Now what would a small town girl like me know about cars? Why don't you come over to my place and I will show you pleasures unlike anything you've ever experienced before?"

I pushed her away and ran out the front door. I stopped dead in my tracks in fear as one of the sirens was standing before me surrounded by twenty other women. They all had seductive smiles on their faces. Vicki walked out the door and over to me. She stood next to me and held my right hand.

"Please, Jake," she said seductively. "Don't worry, she's not going to hurt you."

"What's going on?" I looked at the siren and then back at her.

"She knows I want you. I got tired of Jeff as my husband so I went looking for a new one last night and found you. I called out to the siren and she came to take Jeff away as a sacrifice. We must sacrifice a husband to a siren once every hundred years to receive eternal youth. A small price for immortality."

"You can't do this!"

"Watch."

The siren raised her right hand slowly and rested it on my left shoulder and I suddenly felt no desire to leave. I wanted to stay in Lake Station for the rest of my life. I looked at Vicki. My beautiful Vicki. My dream. My love. My life.

Alien Town

Alice held a gun pointed at the john her and her girlfriend, Tara, had just brought back to the cheap hotel. Tara sat on the bed holding a towel wrapped in ice after their client had punched her in the face.

"What are you going to do, pretty thing? You don't have the balls to pull the trigger," he threatened.

He towered over her and had tattoos all over his arms of famous actresses' faces. He wasn't the type of client they normally entertained, but they were in an unfamiliar town and were desperate for money. He stared at her with a smirk, begging her to pull the trigger.

"Just get out of here. We won't call the cops."

"Now why would I leave? I'm a paying customer. Until I'm completely satisfied, I'm not leaving."

"This is your last chance!" Alice threatened. Perspiration was streaming down her face from the extreme heat from the August sun.

He smiled sinisterly causing her to be more freaked out. She looked over at Tara who was crying. As she relived the encounter — him getting too rough and hitting Tara because she wouldn't let him choke her during sex — the more severe her anger became.

"Maybe you and I should have a go-around," he said, moving closer to her.

She closed her eyes and pulled the trigger.

"You bitch!" he shouted as he fell to the floor.

"You shot him," Tara said in shock as she watched him bleed to death.

Alice dropped the gun and got on her knees. Her hands were trembling and she wanted to say something to Tara, but the words wouldn't come.

"Somebody probably heard the shot. We are not safe here."

Alice looked at her and after a few minutes, calmed herself down. "Tara, we better get out of here before the cops come."

"He's dead." Tara grabbed the gun and handed it to her.

"What's done is done." She stared at the john's body and back at Tara. "It was self-defense."

"It doesn't matter. We're Russian. We're just visiting America. They will probably accuse us of being Russian spies. We don't want them to contact the Russian authorities."

"Tara, that is ridiculous. Just because we're Russian doesn't mean we're spies."

"Alice, tell that to the police when they arrive. Now let's get out of here before they come."

Tara grabbed Alice's hand and helped her to her feet and then grabbed all the money out of the john's wallet. They quickly grabbed their purses and ran for the minivan they rented at the airport.

"Tara, I'll drive. Your face is swelling up. You need to keep ice on it."

"I'll be fine. I've suffered worse injuries from a john before."

"Unfortunately, so have I," she said as she drove the minivan out of the hotel's parking lot. She kept checking the rearview mirror for any flashing lights from a squad car, but so far nothing.

"Alice, slow down. The last thing we need is to be pulled over for speeding."

"You're right," she said and relaxed her foot on the accelerator.

She thought about their move from Russia. They had been entertaining some clients when they heard machine gunfire in one of the mob apartment complexes. One of their clients had hid them out on the balcony of the apartment before two guys slammed the door open and opened fire killing the clients. They had stayed on the balcony until they thought it was safe and climbed down the fire escape. From there, they returned to their apartment in Moscow and grabbed all their money and their passports. They headed for the airport and now they were running because of another dead body. After spending all of their money they made from prostitution and selling several lesbian videos to numerous sex sites, they had resorted to prostitution in the States to get by. The fear that someone from Russia would come after them for witnessing the murder of two of the key men in the Russian mob haunted them, keeping them off the grid. The last thing they needed was to get involved in the homicide of a US citizen.

"Alice, there's an exit coming up. Renovo, Pennsylvania."

"Renovo it is," Alice said as she followed the exit off of the highway. "The first chance we get, we better get some gas and some food. Make sure you are wearing your sunglasses. We don't need to attract any attention."

They drove for a couple hours before seeing a bright neon sign for a gas station and a small diner called Jorel's Diner and Gas Fill-Up Station. After filling up the vehicle, they parked in front of the diner.

"Remember, we're on the run. We're not looking for any clients," Alice cautioned.

"I'll be as innocent as a young school girl," Tara said, managing a slight smile while still feeling a lot of pain from the punch to the face.

"Not a smart way for a prostitute to describe herself, but it will have to do," she said, following her into the diner.

They sat down on two stools by the counter. Alice quickly glanced around the diner making sure there were no cops.

"What would you girls like?" the waitress asked as she was wiping the counter off with a dirty towel.

"Two diet sodas and a couple of burgers and fries," Alice answered.

"Coming right up," the waitress said.

"I think we'll be safe here for now," Alice assured Tara as the waitress walked away.

"We're in the middle of nowhere."

"Which is a good thing, I believe."

In the middle of their conversation, the lights went out in the diner. The whole diner became silent except for a kid who was frightened by the darkness. A huge fireball flew past the diner. A minute later the lights came back on. Some of the diners were looking out the window trying to figure out what they just witnessed.

"Was that a missile?" Tara asked.

"It looked more like a large meteor," Alice answered.

Tara spotted a police car parked in front of the diner.

"Alice, the cops."

Alice glanced around the diner looking for someone who was sitting alone. In the back of the diner sat a tall man with a thick beard wearing a blue flannel shirt. He had thick glasses and looked like someone who they could easily manipulate. She motioned to Tara to follow her and they walked over to his table.

"Excuse me, mister. Can we join you?" Alice asked seductively.

The man turned his attention away from the window and acknowledged her.

"My name is Alice and this is my friend, Tara."

They sat down on the other side of the table.

"My name's Dean. Did you get a good look at the thing that passed by?"

"Barely. I think it was a meteor," Alice said.

"Meteors fall from the sky. That thing flew by in a straight path," Dean explained. "I had this strange feeling something was off about this town when I arrived here."

"Are you a clairvoyant?" Tara asked.

"No, I just can sense when things seem out of the ordinary."

"Sounds like a clairvoyant."

"What brings you to this town?" Alice asked.

"One of my ancestors is buried here. I was looking for his tombstone earlier."

"That's morbid. Why would you be interested in that?" Alice questioned.

"I'm into genealogy. I'm writing a book on my family's lineage. I've been photographing all of their tombstones for the book."

"That's fascinating," Tara said, trying to sound interested. She found it was helpful to tune out people when they were talking about their personal lives. The less she knew about a john, the easier it was for her to sleep with him without getting emotionally attached.

"It is. I've gotten to do a lot of traveling as of late. I've been to places I never knew existed. I've met a lot of interesting people. I can tell from your accents that you are from Russia."

"We are," Tara said.

"We were. We're here on a visa. We were traveling east when we got lost and ended up here in nowhere land," Alice added.

Their attention was drawn to the commotion happening behind them. Somebody was asking everybody if they were getting a signal on their phones. Everybody in the diner was having the same problem.

"Our cable is out, as well," the waitress said checking every station.

The power went out again.

"I think the fireball passing by and the loss of power and cell service is related," Dean suggested. He could see two police officers, holding their flashlights, walking away from the diner. "I think they've spotted something."

Officer Hal Grayson parked the squad car in front of the diner. He looked over at his partner, Damian Drake, who was trying to figure out why the computer in the squad car stopped working.

"What do you expect? The town can barely afford our salaries let alone provide us with reliable equipment," Hal said.

"Dixie, this is Drake. Is your computer working at the station?"

He waited a couple of minutes and looked over at Hal.

"Let me guess, the radio is not working either."

All the hairs on his and Damian's head stood straight up, reminding him of the time he was at the town's science fair and put his hand on a static electric ball. A few seconds later the squad car was filled with a bright yellow light as a large fireball flew past heading toward the forest to the north and crashed.

"What the hell was that?" Damian asked.

"I don't know, but it crashed by old man Kallor's cabin."

"The power in the diner just went out."

"Grab the flashlights out of the glove box. Hopefully, those are still working."

Damian grabbed the flashlights and handed one to Hal who smiled when it actually lit up. They got out of the car and headed for the dirt trail leading into the forest.

"Be on guard. We have no idea what that was," Hal warned.

"I would be more concerned about being shot by a drunken Kallor. He doesn't respond too well to trespassers."

They cautiously continued forward. The forest was extremely quiet. They didn't hear any crickets chirping, making Damian nervous. Up ahead, they could see the cabin.

"Hal, we better stop by and let him know we're out here."

"Probably not a bad idea."

As they drew closer to the cabin, they could see a body lying face first on the porch. They quickly ran for the porch. Hal kneeled down by Kallor's body. He rolled the body over and dropped his flashlight in horror. Kallor's face was completely ripped off exposing his skull. The top of it was ripped open and the brain was missing.

"Hal, excuse me," Damian said and bent over the porch railing and puked.

"Damian, whatever did this may still be out here? Regain your composure."

Damian grabbed his handkerchief and wiped his chin. "How long has he been dead?"

"I'm no coroner. He's still bleeding. This just happened."

"Where's his shotgun?"

Hal shined his flashlight all over the porch and then on the ground in front of the cabin. The shotgun lay on the ground a few feet away from the porch broken into several pieces.

Damian walked over and collected all of the pieces. He laid them on the porch away from the body and inspected each piece, shaking his head in disbelief.

"What?"

"I can't make any sense of this. It looks like something just ripped it apart."

"An animal?"

"Do you think this and the fireball we saw earlier are related?"

Hal walked over the body and grabbed one of the pieces from the ground and inspected it. "If that is the case, then we are in serious trouble. We better get back to the squad car. We are going to need backup."

Damian pulled out his gun as he heard a branch snap nearby. Hal stood up. He could see something dark hunched down in the bushes. He grabbed Damian's arm and pulled him backward toward the cabin's front door. As the dark figure walked out from behind the bushes, he slammed the front door and locked the deadbolt.

"What did you see?" Damian asked.

"I don't think you would believe me."

"What was it?"

"An alien."

"A little green man?"

"It wasn't little and it wasn't green. Its head was shaped like one, but it was grotesque."

They jumped backward as something hit the door so hard the door shook.

"I don't think the door is going to hold. Don't hesitate. Shoot when it breaks through," Hal ordered.

The door forcibly burst inward. A large, grey creature with an overgrown round head and glowing blue eyes rushed into the room so fast it was on top of Hal within seconds, ripping his face off with its razor-sharp claws. Before Damian could fire his gun, the creature ripped his hand completely off. As he screamed, it ripped his face off, as well. It returned its focus on Hal and grabbed the top of his skull and ripped out his brain followed by Damian's. It walked out of the cabin carrying both of their brains. It stopped by the bushes outside the cabin and grabbed Kallor's brain it had dropped on the ground.

The lights came back on in the diner. Alice could see the panic on all the diners' faces.

"Are we safe here?" Tara asked, grabbing Alice's right hand.

"My watch stopped working." Dean showed them his digital watch, which wasn't displaying any numbers. "I bought this on Amazon recently."

One of the diners walked outside toward his car. A couple minutes later he walked back inside complaining his car wouldn't start.

"Miguel, make sure there is plenty of gasoline in the generator," the waitress instructed.

"Yes, Barbara."

Miguel grabbed the gas can from the closet in the storage room and walked out the back door of the diner toward the generator. The generator was humming. He put the gas can down and stared at the panel on the generator. As he was bending down to get a closer look, he could hear something breathing heavily from behind him. As he turned around, the alien creature grabbed the top of his head and ripped his face off. It quickly ripped open his skull, pulled out his brain and then ripped the side of the generator open with one of its claws.

The diner went dark.

"Not again," Alice said nervously.

The creature walked past the front of the diner holding all four of the brains and disappeared into the forest.

"What the hell was that?" Tara watched as the creature disappeared. "We better get out of here."

"Whatever that thing was, it was huge," Dean pointed out.

The waitress screamed loudly as she found Miguel's body outside.

"Wait here," Dean ordered as he ran through the kitchen to see what had transpired. The waitress was standing by the body screaming hysterically. Dean grabbed her shoulders and led her back into the diner, trying to calm her down.

Alice and Tara rushed over to Dean as he helped the waitress sit down on one of the stools. She tried to regain her composure, but the image of Miguel was burned into her mind.

"Blood everywhere," she said hysterically.

"You're safe now," Dean assured her.

"Am I?"

Dean looked at Alice and Tara with a concerned look on his face signaling to them they were all in danger. A woman screamed as the creature was standing outside one of the diner's windows. The creature smashed the window inward, grabbed the woman by the throat and pulled her through the window. Her husband grabbed on to her legs, and then fell backward holding her lower torso after losing a tug of war with the creature who held on to her tightly until her body ripped in half.

Alice pulled the gun out of her right cowboy boot and fired a couple rounds at it. The creature quickly dashed away from the diner and into the forest.

"We better find a place to hide away from here," Tara suggested.

"My hotel is down the road in walking distance," Dean said.

"If we're lucky, we'll find a car there that is working." Alice led them out of the diner ready to fire another round into the creature if they encountered it.

As they followed the road leading in the opposite direction of the forest, they spotted a car that had crashed into a tree. The driver had been flung halfway through the windshield. His head was ripped open with his brain missing.

"Where is his brain?" Tara asked disgusted.

"When I saw it walk past the diner, it was holding four brains," Alice said.

Tara screamed as she saw the creature rushing toward them.

Alice shot the remaining bullets at the creature's head. It fell forward landing in front of them. Alice slammed her boots on its head repeatedly until its greenish blood was gushing everywhere. "That's what you get for messing with a Russian!"

From the distance they could see a large fireball rise above the trees. It hovered in midair for several seconds before it began to head in their direction.

"Run!" Alice shouted, running for the hotel.

The fireball flew past them and crashed into the hotel obliterating it. They stopped running and watched as a creature, twice the size as the one they just killed, walked out of the fiery blaze. It looked over at them and screamed out so loudly they had to cover their ears. It slowly moved toward them limping.

"I think it's hurt," Dean pointed out.

"What do we do?" Tara asked.

"We run back toward the forest," Alice ordered and grabbed her arm.

They ran for the forest as the creature slowly chased after them. They passed the diner where the remaining diners were lying inside dead with their brains removed. They entered the forest and ran until they came to the cabin.

"There may be something inside we can use," Alice suggested and led them inside where the two cops lay dead.

"The carnage," Dean said as he grabbed one of the flashlights off the floor.

They walked into the kitchen where a couple of rifles were sitting on a large gun rack made out of a deer's antlers. Alice handed one to Dean and grabbed the other one. On the table were several boxes filled with bullets.

Tara grabbed an ax which was standing by a stack of firewood.

"Aim for its head," Alice instructed.

They heard a noise coming from the front of the cabin. Alice walked out the kitchen and saw two smaller creatures similar to the one they killed earlier. She shot one of them in the head. The other one ran toward her. Tara swung the ax implanting it into its skull. It fell backward dead.

"How many of them are there?" Alice asked, looking at Tara.

Dean cautiously walked onto the porch.

"Do you see anything?" Alice asked.

Before he could answer, his head was sliced off and it rolled backward into the cabin stopping at Tara's feet. She tried not to vomit as his dead eyes stared up at her.

"Tara, be ready."

The creature slowly walked into the cabin limping with each step. It looked at Alice and opened its mouth exposing all of its large sharp teeth.

"You're not going to scare me that easily," Alice said and fired the rifle. The creature slumped to its knees. She walked over to it. It stared up at her daring her to pull the trigger. She smiled and fired. The alien fell backward. She stomped on its head repeatedly until the floor was covered in its blood.

Tara rushed over to her and put her hands on her shoulders.

"I'm all right," Alice assured her.

"I hope that was the last one."

"Let's not stick around and find out."

They walked out of the cabin and walked away from the town until they reached the interstate, never looking back.

HAUNTED ATTRACTIONS

James stood before the crumbling tombstones of the Marshes Cemetery, a haunted cemetery down by Bloomington, Indiana. He had read a story about this cemetery in his Indiana Guide of Haunted Attractions and wanted to experience its haunting first hand. He could barely make out the names on the tombstones due to the thick moss and plants which had overtaken them over the centuries. There were still a few hours of light left. He wasn't afraid of being there at night. He wanted to take some pictures with his digital camera before it was too dark. He snapped a few photos of each of the remaining tombstones.

A squirrel ran out of one of the bushes and stopped curious about what he was doing. He waived at the squirrel as it ran back into the bushes. He could feel a cold chill causing him to have goosebumps all over his arms. It wasn't from the wind; it was from something else. He turned around, but didn't see anything. As quickly as the sensation began, it stopped. Again, he could feel the heat from the hot summer night. As the sun descended and he could see the stars, he walked out of the cemetery and down the dirt trail leading to the main road where his midnight blue Dodge Neon was parked.

He drove away, stopping at the small convenience store to buy a Pepsi and a king size Reese before returning to his hotel. After eating his snack, he hooked his camera up to his laptop to look at the pictures he had taken. His eyes opened wide as he looked at each picture. In the background of each picture was a white mass that got bigger after each picture he took. He checked the lens on his camera, and there was no dirt or smudges. He continued to look at the pictures using the zoom function on his laptop to make the pictures bigger. As he looked at the last picture he took, he stared in shock. When he made the picture bigger, he could see what appeared to be someone's eyes in the white mass. *Was the ghost that had been haunting the cemetery since it had been first used been there with him the whole time?* He could feel the goosebumps all over his body as he realized he had just encountered a ghost. He uploaded the photos onto his Facebook page with the caption: I just captured a ghost on film. Not too long afterward, people were commenting on the post calling the photos fakes, which didn't bother him since he was used to dealing with skeptics.

    He sat down on the edge of the bed and grabbed the Haunted Attractions book and opened it to the page he had bookmarked the night before. The chapter was about a haunted house in Gary, Indiana, which would be his next stop on his journey to visit every haunted attraction in the United States.

Little Town Flirt

Parker slowly walked down the sidewalk with a knife held tightly in his right hand. He could see Delilah's red brick house in the distance. The closer he got to her house, the more his hatred toward her coursed through his veins. His attention was drawn to a raccoon that stared at him through the unkempt lawn of the abandoned house on the corner of Fifth Street and IN-130 in Wheeler, Indiana. For a brief moment, his hatred subsided and he began to regret his plan to get even with her.

Looking toward her two-story house in the windy night, he recalled the other day at Wheeler High School when she laughed in his face after he asked her out. She walked away from him, still laughing, and told everybody she encountered that Mr. Nobody had the balls to ask a cheerleader out. The whole day people poked fun at him, and he remembered one of the popular girls pointing her finger at him and saying, while trying not to laugh hysterically, "The comic book loving loser thought a cheerleader would actually go out with him."

His anger returned and all thoughts of regretting his decision subsided. He stared at the knife while smiling sinisterly. *Oh yes, the bitch has to die!*

He stopped at the edge of her yard. Her bedroom light was on and he could hear music coming from the room. He didn't see her parents' cars in the driveway. *Good, she's all alone.*

He thought about how everyday she wore a tight tank-top and shorts, displaying her perfectly tanned body and teasing everybody around her with her flawless skin. She was constantly twisting her long, raven black hair with her fingers. The constant "you can't have me, but I'm going to flaunt it in your face" look she possessed drove him absolutely insane. Deep down he loved her and didn't understand why a guy like him didn't stand a chance with a girl like her. It wasn't fair. He deserved her.

He thought about yesterday when he was walking down the hallway near the gymnasium and heard her say "Hey handsome, in here."

She was standing in front of the woman's bathroom and was signaling him to follow her inside. As he walked into the bathroom, she pushed him against the mirror and kissed him seductively. She took a step backward and laughed.

"Do you really think I was going to make out with you? You are such an idiot. I've dated every jock that goes to Wheeler. Why would I stoop so low? I may be a whore, but not that type of whore."

She skipped out of the bathroom, slamming the door behind her. He could hear her laughing as she walked down the hallway. As tears formed in his eyes, he stared at his reflection in the mirror. Sadness had quickly disappeared replaced by rage.

Now he stood in front of her house with a knife in his hand ready to exact his revenge. He walked up to her front door and slowly turned the doorknob. To his surprise, it was unlocked. The music coming from her room was very loud. He smiled knowing she wouldn't be able to hear him coming. He cautiously walked up the stairs. As he reached the top of his stairs, he readied his knife for the attack. He walked up to her door, which had a sign that said "Princess" taped to it. He laughed because there was no way she would ever be accused of being a princess.

He slowly pushed the door open. She was sitting at her desk in front of her laptop facing away from the door.

He held the knife sideways ready to slit her throat. As he grabbed one of her shoulders, her head fell forward hard onto the laptop. The laptop, desk, and carpet were covered in blood and it looked fresh. He lifted up her head and her throat was slit, and there were several stab wounds all over her body.

His anger was quickly replaced with sadness. Someone else had exacted revenge on his love before he could. He held her in his arms and cried.

With the music from her radio blasting loudly, he didn't hear the police sirens approaching or the police running up the stairs toward her room.

"Drop the knife!"

Holding her tightly, he looked back toward the two police officers who were pointing their weapons toward him.

Covered in her blood, he dropped the knife and said, "I didn't kill her."

Master of Discontent

I'm not sure when I arrived, but I'll never forget my stay.

When I found myself in a large cavern, the odorous scent of the brimstone stung sharply in my nostrils. I staggered to my feet, but was immediately forced back to my knees by a large cloud of burnt sulfur gas. When my bloodshot eyes had adjusted to the dimness, I was able to survey the rocky environment. It consisted of rock and active volcanic fire. My position was near the base of an underground cliff. The sheer drop was approximately eighty meters. The ceiling was perhaps three hundred meters above me. It formed a dome at least ten kilometers around. The length extended as far in either direction as could be seen. Scattered within were countless stalagmites and stalactites. Some of the former were burning fiercely and eternally. It was these stalagmites that illuminated the chamber.

"Good eternity!" boomed a guttural voice behind me. "I'm your host! You may address me as Mephistopheles!"

I whirled around and there through the fading mist I glimpsed a tall mysterious man. "Welcome to my humble abode. I hope you will enjoy your visit. And now, if you will follow me…"

His voice trailed off. I must admit, I was dumfounded. This Mephistopheles was a tall, immobile figure. He was wearing a hooded, black cloak and black Russian Cossack boots. A gold link chain fastened with a silver inlay dagger was around his waist.

"Silver," he remarked, "is sometimes necessary in controlling our more excitable guests. You shall be assigned to rock and coke detail. Quarry Eight. Since you had a flawless record on Midgard, you are hereby appointed Quarry Master. You're quite lucky. Most new arrivals are made into carriers."

We walked along for a couple of yards when an anguished scream rippled through the heavy silence. Acting as though nothing had happened, my new master continued on the journey toward the mysterious Quarry Eight. Suddenly, another scream rang out. Seeing I was becoming more and more cautious, my companion began to chuckle.

At last, we came to our dismal destination. A more retched place can't be imagined. The entrance was nothing more than a three meter square opening in the wall. From it a slope led downward at an acute thirty degree angle. The walls were encrusted with fungus and large splotches of algae. Here and there on the floor were puddles of green slime. An odor of decay heightened the air of despair.

Then I saw the slave carriers. My God, the carriers were beaten ad starved wretches. Driven to the limits of the unknown, these ragged and forlorn beasts of burden were more animal than humans they vaguely resembled.

I was to direct these spiritless zombies? My stomach fought to upsurge and I gurglingly lost the battle into the pits. I must find Mephistopheles and demand to be freed from this monstrous chamber of horrors.

Receiving jumbled instructions, I slowly made my way out. I hadn't trekked long when I began to wish I had never started out. I began running and then I saw I was involved in some odd cat and mouse game. And I was the prey.

Following me was a new, unspeakable, nameless horror. Three large, red-eyed bats, dripping red liquid from their slit-like mouths were silently winging above.

Exhausted, I stumbled past other souls lost in time, other decaying ruined mines, and pools of sulfuric slime. Finally, I picked up a huge rock and braced myself to meet my tormentor.

A huge mastiff with three foaming heads appeared before me. Was this to be the last thing I'd ever see?

Suddenly, a cloud of acid smoke engulfed us both. It passed quickly revealing that Mephistopheles had joined us. With a wave of his clawed hand, the mastiff and bats slithered off.

"Why didn't you remain at the quarry?" he thundered.

My head ached severely and I felt a warm ooze trickling down my neck. I probed and found a large hole in the back of my head about the size of a bullet. My mind throbbed painfully. I felt pushed to inhuman limits.

"In the name of God! What is this place to harbor such horrors as these?"

"Surely you remember. Or has amnesia set upon your mind?" he said as the truth began to glimmer in my brain. "Suicides are eternally damned to burn!"

"I remember trying to kill myself," I screamed, "but I don't remember anything else after that until I woke up here. Just where in the hell am I?"

"You see, my friend," he said, laughing hideously, "that is exactly where you are!"

Silently, I went back with Mephistopheles following behind me to Quarry Eight to work for all eternity.

The Kick

Marty watched as the clowns jumped out of the tiny compact car one after another after another after another. He loved going to the carnival down in Connersville, Indiana. This year they added a circus attraction. He had never seen an elephant up close before and this year he finally had his chance. His younger sister, Lois, laughed as the clowns collided into each other as one of them suddenly stopped to avoid crashing into one of the large elephants.

Marty's mom laughed. He had never witnessed his mom having so much fun before. He never could have imagined the circus would bring his mother so much joy. *Maybe becoming a clown would be a great career choice. Besides, anybody could be a fireman or an astronaut.* He turned his attention back toward the clowns as one of them sprayed the others with a seltzer bottle.

After the show, they sat down at the picnic tables set up near the small food trucks and ate hot dogs while their mom ate an elephant ear. After they were done eating, their mom gave them some money to play some of the carnival games while she rested. His sister tried throwing metal hoops onto some bottles while he threw some darts at some balloons in the hope of winning a small square mirror with the Superman emblem on it. After finally winning one after spending several dollars, he walked away to rejoin his sister. He could see her still unsuccessfully throwing the hoops. As he got closer to her, somebody grabbed him and dragged him behind one of the trailers.

"Let go of me!" Marty said as he struggled to get free.

"Be quiet or I'll cut you," the man threatened. He was a tall man dressed in raggedy clothes. He had a cigar in his mouth and looked like he hadn't shaved in a couple of weeks. Marty had seen the guy many times during the day. He apparently had been following them the whole time waiting for his chance to grab him. "You're going to come with me, or I will go after your sister. And trust me, you don't want me to do that."

Marty stopped struggling.

"Good," the man said. Before he could say another word, Marty kicked him hard in the crotch. He fell to the ground screaming in pain.

Marty ran toward his sister. As he ran, he remembered two years ago when his uncle had taught him to protect himself. He had warned him of the dangers of strangers, and that his feet could be one of the best weapons he could possess from being abducted. His uncle, a black belt in karate, taught him everything he knew about karate. Today, those skills came in handy.

Games

    Malcolm's heart beat faster and faster as he was lying in the bushes waiting for the games to begin. He looked over at Brayden and asked, "How long do we have to wait for the games to begin?"

    Brayden was dressed in a beige military uniform smeared with dried blood. He had a brown bandana soaked with sweat covering his bald head. He had a couple scars on his face from many fights he had been in over the years. He looked annoyed as he stared at Malcolm wearing his clean blue t-shirt and blue jeans advertising he was a rookie to the games.

    "Since this is your first time, Malcolm, it just might be all day."

    "All day! There are plenty of things I'd rather be doing at home than this."

    "What? Read your so-called comic books." He and his friend, Colton, laughed at him for several seconds before returning their gaze to the field in front of them.

    Malcolm stood up angrily and walked toward his friend, Tyler, who had talked him into participating in the games.

    "Get down, you idiot, before you give away our position," somebody whispered.

    Kneeling down next to Tyler, Malcolm asked, "Why did I ever let you talk me into this?"

    "Because you are my best friend."

    Looking down the little hill they were on and straight ahead into the green meadows with trees and bushes, Malcolm thought about the corrupt direction the world had gone in. To him, the games signified how stupid humans had gotten. The games were created to keep degenerate men off the streets. He wasn't as bad as Tyler, but wondered if a part of him was as psychotic as those surrounding him. He was the only one there he knew who didn't have a criminal record. His friend had been in and out of jail several times for selling narcotics. Brayden had killed a police officer while fleeing a bank robbery. Colton had murdered his wife and the guy he caught her banging in his bed when he came home a couple hours early from work.

When the government had banned the Bible and burned down all the churches fifty years prior, the world began to follow the devil's path. All the Christians were sentenced to death as in the Roman times when Christians were fed to the lions.

But even in the darkest times, there were a few beautiful souls left in the world. Malcolm's wife had been one. She had the courage to stand up against the government and publically damn them to hell. When they came for her, he didn't have the guts to stand by her and admit she was his wife or say that he believed in God. He told them he divorced her three months prior because of her beliefs. The look on her face when he betrayed her was permanently burned into his mind and ever since that day, he prayed daily to God and to her for their forgiveness.

He didn't want to participate in the games, but Tyler had finally convinced him after weeks of going on about how it was for a good cause. He never told him what they would be hunting, just that it was the best prize any serious hunter could want.

"Gents, get your guns ready for our prize is coming," Brayden instructed.

Over the bushes, they could see their prey. Behind one of the trees, several Christian women wearing ripped clothing and shoes that had been worn through, stood looking around nervously. They had been imprisoned for several months until it was their turn to be hunted during the games.

He looked at them in shock? Humans were the game? Was he at the point when he degraded himself to the level of an animal hunting a helpless prey? With his guilt heavy on his soul, why would he willingly agree to get involved in this madness? Everybody, but him, ran down the hill ready to toy with the women until the men were ready to torture and kill them.

Tyler turned around and looked at him. "Aren't you coming?"

"If Donna could see me now?"

"She's dead. Killed by the government because she was foolish enough to believe in God. There is no God." He looked over at the women running for their lives. "Man, they are such a beautiful prize!"

As Tyler was running away to join the game, Malcolm shot him in the back of the head with his rifle. Tyler fell down. Malcolm walked over to Tyler and watched him bleed out.

"I'm sorry, my friend; I can't be a part of this," he said as his friend died.

Malcolm stood up and stared at the other men hunting the women. With a determined look on his face, he ventured onto the field to hunt the ones who were on the hunt. The women would be no prize for these men. No longer would he stand idly by and watch a Christian being slaughtered.

Where Evil Shall Dwell

April 13, 1964

"Sub-Mariner to base! Sub-Mariner to base. Proceeding along as planned. About one hundred miles west to southwest of Bermuda. Should we stay on course?"

"Roger, Sub-Mariner. Just proceed as planned. No deviations. Over and out," the radio operator instructed.

"Captain, can I ask a few questions about this experiment?" Ira Labanowski asked, listening intently to the conversation.

"Ira, you may."

"How does this involve me and what is this experiment going to prove?"

"Ira, there is an area from Jacksonville, Florida to Puerto Rico, from Puerto Rico to Bermuda and from Bermuda to Jacksonville that is called the Bermuda Triangle also known as the triangle of death."

"Bermuda triangle?" Ira asked.

"There have been between one hundred and two hundred ships and planes since 1945 that have vanished or been destroyed by someone or something between these coordinates outlined on my map. We don't have the slightest clue to their whereabouts and, worst of all, the United States government is pressuring us to find the truth behind this mystery. Several of our allies want answers since they also have lost ships. We've heard about your experience with the James Charlot case and how you used your sixth sense to crack it."

"I'm not sure if my psychic abilities can be much use in this matter." Ira sat there and thought about the events that led to him being hired by the United States government and being transported via helicopter to the small radio shack in Fort Jackson. His colleague, a senator, offered him a hefty paycheck to advise the captain about the experiment, but didn't give him any specifics. He remembered hearing a radio newscast about a British ship on training maneuvers disappearing and Britain claiming it was destroyed by a US Naval vessel days before. "Have you tried this experiment before?"

"Yes, three times without success. This time, with your help, we hope it will be successful."

Ira felt like he was having a migraine attack. He closed his eyes to shield them from the bright light and saw the Sub-Mariner in a dense fog. He couldn't see anything through the fog and then the plane vanished. He opened his eyes and looked at the captain. "The plane is in trouble. It has lost all sense of direction."

"Captain, I'm picking up a faint transmission," the radio operator reported.

"Sub-Mariner to base!" an exhausted voice came over the intercom.

"Turn on the tape recorder!" the captain ordered.

The radio operator turned on the tape recorder as the voice continued. "Help! We're lost! Lost all sense of direction. Don't know which way is north, south, east or west!"

"Do you have any idea where you are?" The radio operator asked.

"Smack in the middle of nowhere."

"Contact Star Duster," the captain ordered.

"Base to Star Duster! Base to Star Duster! Sub-Mariner is in trouble. They are lost somewhere between Bermuda and here at Fort Jackson. Over."

"Roger, base. We're on our way."

A couple of seconds later, the voice of the pilot of the Sub-Mariner could be heard. "I'm feeling very dizzy like I'm experiencing vertigo."

"Do you know what is causing this?" the radio operator asked.

"I don't know. Wow, you have to see this. The sky is a darkish green. Even the ocean doesn't look right. There's no sun. It appears to be nighttime."

"Impossible. It's three o'clock in the afternoon," the captain said, looking over at Ira.

"Nothing is impossible when dealing with the unknown," Ira advised.

"Base to Sub-Mariner! Base to Sub-Mariner! Come in! Do you hear us, Sub-Mariner? Come in!" The radio operator looked at the captain who was also concerned.

Ira closed his eyes and saw the plane floating in midair in complete darkness. He could see the pilot. His eyes were closed and his head slumped forward. "The pilot's dead."

The captain was about to respond when he was interrupted by the co-pilot's voice. "The pilot is dead. I felt this coldness go through me and then the pilot grabbed his chest and spit up blood. His eyes rolled back in his head and he slumped forward."

Ira closed his eyes and saw a translucent hand enter the pilot's chest and squeeze his heart until it burst. "Captain, he was murdered."

"Murdered? By whom?"

"I don't know. It's all so blurry."

"Oh no! Get away!" the co-pilot screamed. "Get away!"

"I lost contact with the Sub-Mariner," the radio operator reported.

"He's dead," Ira said sadly.

"Ira, can you see anything?" the captain asked.

Ira closed his eyes. He could only see complete darkness. "My vision of the scene is dark and blurry."

The radio operator screamed, grabbed his head and fell to the floor. The captain ran over to him and checked his pulse. "He's dead."

Ira kneeled down next to him and examined his body. "Judging by the look on his face, he was frightened to death."

"Huh?" The captain looked at him puzzled.

Ira closed his eyes and saw through the radio operator's eyes what had scared him to death. The radio operator's deceased mother, disfigured and covered in maggots walking toward him screaming in German to stay away.

Ira looked at the captain. "It was a warning to stay away from the Bermuda triangle."

"We better warn the Star Duster!"

As the captain was standing up, the north wall collapsed. As the dust settled, he reached for the radio. "Base to Star Duster! Base to Star Duster! Turn Back! Do not approach the Bermuda triangle!"

"Roger, base….What the hell is that? Oh no! It's coming right for us! Get Away! Get Away! No!"

As they heard cries for help through the radio, the rest of the walls collapsed inward burying them. The captain pushed Ira under the table in time as the ceiling crashed downward.

The last thing Ira heard before he passed out was a booming voice through the radio saying, "If someone with your physic abilities ever interferes with me again, the whole world will face my wrath."

Ira regained consciousness several minutes later. The captain was dead with a frightened look on his face. Ira pulled himself out of the rubble and looked up. He could see the sky above him through the gigantic hole in the ceiling. The sky was a darkish green.

The Dogs

My gun was ready and I slowly looked around the corner of the building toward the back door waiting for my prey. A prey I'm getting paid to kill. You see, I'm a hitman — somebody who gets paid thousands to kill people. Nice business to get into if you have a knack for it. One thing, just don't get caught doing it.

John Lumm, you're going to wish you hadn't double crossed your ex-business partner like you did, because, baby, your destiny is now in my hands.

It's a dog eat dog world and that is why I take these types of assignments. I hate greedy souls who reap thousands of dollars at the expense of the misery of others.

I tried other jobs, but just couldn't find any enjoyment in them. I don't like other people ordering me around. I just want to be by myself: working at my own pace and leisure.

I first tried being a salesman for a couple of months, but I felt like I was cheating people by selling them cheap products which they didn't really need. I then tried selling life insurance for almost six months. I got into it with the district manager when the company wouldn't pay the death claims.

It was as a bartender in Las Vegas where I met Arthur Hamlin, a former hitman. I knew him for a year before he revealed what he used to do. From then on, I was hooked because it gave me the sense of adventure I was looking for.

"Why?" some people asked. I don't know.

Suddenly, I heard a click from the screen door. I gripped the silencer tightly. Slowly, the door opened and it was him. The one and only double crosser himself.

As I approached him, I said, "Mr. Lumm, I suggest in your next life you don't cheat your partner."

"What! No!" he screamed.

I fired my gun. The bullet struck him in his heart. I thought it was ironic since I didn't know businessmen had hearts. I whirled around, replaced the gun in my jacket, and darted straight toward my aero car when somebody ran out of the same house yelling, "Somebody stop him! He killed my husband!"

I ran faster. Finally reaching the aero car, I jumped in and pressed my finger on the ignition pad. Seconds later, the car lifted off the ground several feet and I gunned the bloody thing out of the area.

"The dogs are going to get you for what you did back there," a voice coming from the backseat said.

I looked in the rearview mirror and saw somebody in the backseat.

"How in the hell did you get in here?" I asked.

"There isn't an aero car I can't break into. Their security system can easily be hacked."

"Why are you in my car?" I asked annoyed.

"I'm tagging along for a ride. Don't try anything funny. I have a gun pointed at your back," he said, laughing.

A few minutes later he climbed into the front seat while holding the gun toward me. "My name's Mike. What is yours?"

"My name is Jake."

"Interesting. Mighty interesting." He stared at me for a few minutes and then asked, "You love killing people? It gives you a personal thrill?"

"I only kill certain people. People who love to see other lives in misery — like corporate people. I get hired by people who want them removed. If they have the money, I do the service."

For the next hour, I tried to think of some way to get rid of him. I suddenly remembered him saying the dogs were going to get me. I looked over at him and asked, "What did you mean about the dogs?"

"My parents always told me when I did something bad the dogs would be coming for me. If you commit the ultimate sin, they will appear. I've always believed they made it up to keep me in line."

Out of the blue he said, "I could use the company of a woman. All nice and tight."

I gave him a disapproving look.

"So how much?"

"How much for what?"

"How much to kill my parents?"

"I only kill those who deserve it."

"I'm just joking. You don't need to be so serious."

Again, I gave him a disapproving look.

A few minutes later, I saw a young woman up ahead standing beside the road thumbing for a ride. Mike leaned forward and then said, "Stop. Pick her up."

"No."

"I think you will." I felt the gun being pushed into my ribs. I slowed the car down and landed it by the side of the road where the woman was standing. Mike pressed the button lowering his window.

"Where are you both headed?" she asked.

"We're heading to Connersville," Mike answered.

"Great. It's in my direction."

She was beautiful. She had brown hair and brown eyes and a great slender figure. She wore cut of blue jeans with a red checkered tank top.

"What's your name?" Mike asked.

"Nancy."

"Mine is Mike and my friend here is Jake." He slid the door open and climbed out pointing his gun at her.

She took a couple steps backward trembling with fear.

"Jake, give me your gun or I'll be forced to shoot this fine lady."

I looked at her for a few seconds and then handed him my gun.

"Do not leave unless you want me to kill her. I'll be back when I have my way with her."

"Please don't," she pleaded.

"I'm sorry, my dear, but somebody as hot as you shouldn't be hitchhiking."

Mike looked at me for a second and grabbed her by the hair and dragged her into the bushes. I climbed out the car watching him drag her away. There was no way I was going to let him kill her let alone have his way with her. I moved around the car when suddenly I had the strange feeling I was being watched. I heard a branch break from the other side of the road. I could hear Nancy screaming and the sound of a struggle. I ran through the bushes as Mike was slapping her across the face. I ran toward him and he pointed his gun toward me.

"Another move and you're dead," he threatened.

"You're an animal!" I yelled.

Nancy's shirt was ripped and she was staring at me crying.

Mike walked past me pointing the gun at my head. "You can stay with her. I'm taking your car."

As I got near her, she stood up and yelled, "I hope the dogs get you both!"

I heard a branch break behind me.

"The dogs are here!" she yelled angrily.

I heard more branches break.

"They're going to get you," she said, staring at me. Her body began to glow bright blue. Her body transformed from a human into a large white dog.

From the distance, I heard Mike screaming. I slowly backed away from her and then ran faster than I ever had before. I pushed through the bushes and saw Mike lying on the ground in a pool of his own blood. I ran toward my car and jumped in. I pressed my finger on the ignition pad and the car lifted several feet and then crashed to the ground. I looked in the rearview mirror and saw a gigantic black dog holding onto to my bumper with its teeth. I slammed my foot on the accelerator with no success. In front of me was another dog growling while another ripped the roof completely off. I looked up and saw one of the dogs staring down at me. I felt its hot breath and a few seconds later it grabbed me with its sharp teeth.

The dog dropped me onto the ground, and I saw the white dog walk out of the bushes.

"Do you fear the dogs now?" the white dog asked. She lowered her head motioning to the other dogs to attack. As they ripped me to shreds, I lost consciousness.

When I opened my eyes, I was in my car. Mike was pointing his gun at me.

Mike leaned forward and then said, "Stop. Pick her up."

I could see Nancy standing by the side of the road. I looked over at Mike and slammed on the brakes. He pulled the trigger. I felt a pain in my chest as the bullet penetrated my heart. I grabbed my gun from out of my jacket and shot him in the head.

Mike was dead and soon I will be too.

Travelers

Valparaiso, IN

Dave watched as the birds ate all the bread he had thrown from the park bench. From behind him, he could hear a girl playfully giggle. He turned around and watched a young couple rolling around in the grass. He shook his head. He turned his attention back to the birds. He thought about the time back in high school when Jack, Lonnie, and he had gone to the drive-in movie to pick up some girls. Jack and Lonnie had found a couple of cute girls for themselves but not for him, which was just how his luck with women always had been. He could never find anyone interested in a loner like himself. He wasn't someone who could ever be a cover model for GQ magazine. For what women looked for in a man, he was way below average. His hair receded when he was in his teens and now, in his sixties, he still hadn't found anyone. Every now and then, the loneliness would overtake him making his heart ache for someone to love him. The sound from the young couple giggling snapped him out of his deep thought.

"Get a room," he mumbled.

The couple, while holding hands, walked out of the park, and he watched them drive away in a black corvette. He resumed his bird watching. Suddenly, all of the birds flew away as if something had just startled them. He looked around expecting to see some cat trying to make one of the birds its afternoon snack, but he didn't see any predators lurking around anywhere. He could smell something foul in the air reminding him about the time he returned from a trip to Russia. He won the trip for being a top salesman for the insurance company he worked for. He opened up the refrigerator and found the eggs had become rotten because the refrigerator stopped working while he was away.

He was blinded as he was engulfed in a large ball of bright yellow light. He was knocked to the ground as someone collided into him.

"Garth, watch where you are going!" someone shouted.

"How was I supposed to know the tranzer would put me where someone was standing," Garth said. He grabbed Dave's arm and helped him to his feet. "Sorry. It wasn't intentional."

"Don't mention the tranzer. No one here would understand it," a woman said.

Dave stared at the man wearing a shiny, metallic uniform as his eyes adjusted to the bright light. He looked like he was from some science fiction movie from the fifties.

"Mom should be coming through any second now," the woman said.

Through the light, an older woman with long, dark hair with blonde highlights appeared. She was wearing a shiny, metallic dress.

"Melinda, where's Marty?" Garth asked.

"He didn't make it. He gave his life so we could transport through the tranzer," the older woman said. She looked at Dave suspiciously. "Who is this?"

"He was here when we jumped through," the woman said.

"My name is Dave," he said. He looked at the four in shock. They all were wearing shiny, metallic clothing. His first thought was they had appeared through some type of gateway from the future.

"My name is Melinda. These are my two sons, Garth and Jepkins. This is my daughter, Kendra."

"Are you from the future?" Dave asked.

"That depends. Is this the past?" Jepkins asked. He was muscular and had spiked, blond hair. He had tattoos running down both of his arms.

"Jepkins, it's not nice answering a question with a question," Garth said. He was a husky man with reddish hair. He was shorter than Jepkins with thick glasses reminding Dave of something a nerd would wear. "We can't answer that question. We're not even sure where or when we are."

"Valparaiso, Indiana. 2015," Dave answered.

"We are definitely in the past," Kendra said. She had long, curly, blonde hair with reddish highlights. She was very short and looked like she could be in her early twenties.

"I suggest a memory wipe." Garth pulled out a small device that looked like a cross between a smart phone and a laser gun.

Dave stepped backward in fear.

"Garth, stop," Melinda ordered. "He looks harmless. Besides, we are unfamiliar with this timeframe. We'll need a guide to survive. Will you help us?"

Dave looked over at Garth and then at Melinda. "I have nothing on my plate as of right now."

"I'm assuming that is how they say yes in this timeframe," Kendra said.

"I would suggest ditching the metal outfits. Devo hasn't been popular since the eighties. I suggest getting some clothes at the Goodwill. I'll drive you there and on the way you can tell me how you ended up here," Dave said.

"Thank you," Melinda said as Dave led them toward his vehicle.

"What's Devo?" Garth asked, looking at Kendra who shrugged her shoulders.

Edwards Air Force Base
Area 51, Nevada

Sergeant Malcom Teller watched as their latest secret aircraft, J'onn 6, successfully landed after its first test run. The craft was designed based on the alien spacecraft that crashed in Roswell back in 1947. They had developed several different aircrafts based on that technology over the years, but the J'onn 6 was the crowning achievement. It was the first aircraft that could successfully leave Earth without the need of heavy rockets launching it into space. In theory, it was fast enough to reach Pluto in a matter of days instead of taking unmanned spacecraft twelve years.

"Thing of beauty isn't it?" Mason Parsons, the lead scientist on the J'onn 6 project, asked.

"Yes, it is."

It was a very large spacecraft ten times the size of any of the other crafts on the base. There was room for at least eight people in it. It was designed for long exploratory missions. Personally, Malcom thought it was too cramped in there and couldn't imagine traveling long distances in it.

"Imagine the solar systems we can visit thanks to its speed."

"We first have to launch it into space. Anything can happen. If something goes wrong up there, it could take us years to retrieve it," Malcom said.

"I know it's a gamble, but one worth taking."

"Mason, I agree with you on that point. Unfortunately, our investors aren't interested in a failed mission. This mission has to be a success. There's too much riding on it financially."

"It will. I have faith."

"Faith from a scientist?"

"Even a scientist can have faith."

"We need more than a miracle if we want the funding to continue." Malcom walked over to the craft as the pilot exited the hatch on the top. "How did it handle?"

"Sergeant, it purred like a kitten," Russell White said as he climbed down the side of the craft.

"Sergeant! Sergeant! Sergeant!"

Malcom turned around as Wayne Harris ran down the hallway leading to the hanger. He stopped in front of him trying to catch his breath.

"What is so urgent you're about to have a heart attack from running like a madman?" Malcom asked.

"The satellites just picked up a massive energy spike," Wayne said, still out of breath.

"Where?"

"Valparaiso, IN."

Valparaiso, IN

"These shall do fine," Melinda said as Dave handed her several dresses off of the rack in the Goodwill.

Several people were staring at them.

"We just got back from a sci-fi convention," Dave said loudly. "Go back to what you're doing."

"Thanks again for helping us," Melinda said as she grabbed several dresses for her daughter. "Kendra, you'll look cute in these."

"Really, mom, flowers. When have you ever seen me in flowers?"

"Kendra, we have to blend in."

"I found several flannel shirts for your sons," Dave said. "I hope they are ok out there in my van."

"They're checking the database from this timeframe. Hopefully they can find a way to send us back to our time."

"Melinda, why did you come to my time anyway?" Dave asked.

"Our compound was under attack. By whom, we don't know. If it wasn't for our friend, Marty, we would have never been able to escape in time. We didn't have time to adjust the year to travel back to. This is where the tranzer decided to send us for some reason."

"Why go back to it then?"

"We're planning on traveling back before the attack and hopefully stop it from happening," Kendra answered.

"Do you have a plan?"

"Hopefully, Garth and Jepkins can come up with one. I think we have enough clothing. Can you afford all of these?"

"Trust me, with their prices, this is nothing."

After paying for the clothing, they walked outside and over to the van. Garth had the passenger window down and was waiving at them.

"Did you find something?" Melinda asked.

"I think I found a way home," he answered excitedly.

"That's good news," Dave said.

"There's a problem. This won't be easy. Dave, do you know how to get to Edwards Air Force's remote base in Nevada?"

"Area 51?" Dave looked at him stunned. He knew he was getting himself involved in a suicide mission. "You just don't walk onto that base."

"That's why we need to come up with a clever plan. We'll discuss it on the way there," Garth said.

Melinda stared at David with a look which made his heart almost melt. "I guess we're going to Nevada. We better stop and get something to eat first. We have a couple of days drive ahead of us."

Edwards Air Force Base
Area 51, Nevada

"What do you think could have caused an energy spike of that magnitude?" Malcom asked.

"Sir, I'm not sure." Wayne stared at the computer screen sorting through all the data the satellite had transmitted. "I have a drone en route to Valparaiso. I hope that whatever the source of the energy spike is it's still there and we can find it."

"Imagine the possibilities if we could harness that type of energy," Mason said, looking at the data on his laptop. "The energy there could be the key to making the J'onn 6 go even farther into space at a faster speed."

"Then finding this energy source is a top priority. Wayne, contact Agent Venable and send his team to Valparaiso. Have them poke around and see if anybody witnessed anything out of the ordinary," Malcom commanded.

"Right away." Mason rushed out of the room.

Malcom looked out the window of the conference room toward the J'onn 6 sitting in the hangar below. He looked back over at Wayne who was on the phone with the mission control center at NASA. He looked concerned.

"Wayne, what's wrong?"

"Jennifer Perez at NASA just informed me the energy readings the satellites picked up match the ones we detected in 1947 before the spacecraft crashed in Roswell."

"Put the base on high alert," Malcom ordered. "I'm going to contact the Pentagon."

"Sir?"

"I think we have some unwanted visitors," he said as he rushed out of the conference room.

Queen's Diner
Outside of Chicago

"They won't let us onto the air base. It's a government installation, not a tourist attraction," Dave warned as he bit into a potato wedge.

"That's not the plan. I found a conspiracy theorist website that had an article about a top secret spacecraft spotted flying around Area 51. There is a sketch of the spacecraft and it's definitely the tranzer. This must be the year the tranzer went fully operational, which is why it transported us to this timeframe. I can hack into its system using your tablet and pilot it out of the base and directly to us," Garth explained.

"How did it end up in your timeframe?" Dave asked.

"On the tranzer's first mission, it traveled far out of our solar system and hit a ripple in the space time continuum and ended up in our timeframe, 2684. Our scientists were able to develop a way to make time travel possible from the data it collected. It sits in a hangar at our compound and when it's activated, it spins around at a speed so fast it creates a gateway through time."

"That is why we think the compound was attacked. Our enemies wanted possession of the tranzer," Jepkins said.

"If they took control of your compound, wouldn't they be able to travel through time also?" Dave asked

"It will take time for them to figure out how to use the tranzer, which gives us a few days to complete our mission. We are going to travel to a few hours before the compound was attacked. We will have our forces defeat whoever was behind the attack. We'll need to fly the tranzer out of the solar system and through that ripple in the space time continuum. I've memorized the data it collected on that mission when I was at the compound. I'm sure I can travel its exact course. For this to work, our future selves still have to travel back in time and encounter you, Dave," Garth explained.

"Sounds like we'll be in an endless time travel loop," Kendra pointed out.

"Unless this doesn't work," Jepkins said.

"It will," Melinda assured. "Garth's plans always do."

Edwards Air Force Base
Area 51, Nevada

"Sir, I think you should see this YouTube video someone from Valparaiso recently posted," Wayne suggested.

Malcom stood behind Wayne as he played the video. It was filmed off of someone's cell phone. He could see two females in silver metallic uniforms grabbing clothes off of a rack. An older, balding gentleman, wearing a blue flannel shirt and black slacks, was handing a dress to one of the females.

"Can you enhance the audio?" Malcom asked.

"Yes. Give me a second. Let's replay it."

"Our compound was under attack. By whom, we don't know. If it wasn't for our friend, Marty, we would have never been able to escape in time. We didn't have time to adjust the year to travel back to. This is where the tranzer decided to send us for some reason."

"Why go back to it then?"

"We're planning on traveling back before the attack and hopefully stop it from happening," Kendra answered.

"Do you have a plan?"

"Hopefully, Garth and Jepkins can come up with one. I think we have enough clothing. Can you afford all of these?"

"Time travelers?" Malcolm ordered him to replay the video. After watching it a second time, he leaned over Wayne's shoulder. "Pull up the files from Roswell 1947. I want to see the clothing the pilot was wearing."

Wayne turned toward him in shock after looking at the photos from the Roswell files. "They are wearing the same clothing!"

"I know."

"I'm confused. I thought little green men were piloting the spacecraft that crashed."

"No, Wayne, it is what the government wanted people to believe. The pilot was actually human."

"Human?"

"Apparently from the future. Which means the ship from Roswell had the ability to travel through time." Malcom looked at the paused video. "Run the facial recognition software and get me a name on the guy who was with them."

"Yes, sir."

After a couple of hours of running the facial recognition software, the computer matched his image with the image from the Indiana BMV database. Wayne rushed out of the conference room and into Malcom's office. "I have a name."

"Who is he?"

"Dave Alexander. He drives a green 2010 Ford E-Series Van. He recently used his debit card at the Queen's Diner outside of Chicago."

"Check all the traffic cams around the diner. Maybe one of them picked up his van. Have our team head toward Chicago. Once we have a visual on the van, send the drone to follow it. We need to know where they are heading," Malcolm ordered.

Valparaiso, Indiana

Agent Rick Venable watched two older women walk on the sidewalk at the Bicentennial Park in Valparaiso, Indiana. A large family was having a party at the shelter in the middle of the park. He was checking the radiation levels with his small Geiger meter while Agent Marilyn Austin stood next to him. They were both dressed in blue t-shirts and sweats and also wearing sunglasses to blend in with the rest of the people at the park. Even with her reddish hair tied back in a ponytail, she still looked like she was a federal agent.

"Radiation levels are a little high, but nothing to cause alarm." He kneeled down pretending to tie his left shoe and inspected the grass that had a black outline from being burnt by something. "I think this was made by the source of the energy surge."

"The black outline goes all the way over here," Marilyn said as she followed the black outline toward the backside of the park. "Whatever it was, it was massive."

Rick snapped a few pictures of the ground and emailed them to Malcolm. A few seconds later his phone rang. "Malcolm, yes we are at its location. Time travel? If what you say is true, we're standing where they came through. No, there are no traffic cameras around the park. The park is away from the main road. Yes, sir."

Marilyn walked over to him, trying to listen in on the conversation. As he ended the call, he looked at her puzzled. "Apparently, we are dealing with time travelers."

"What's our next move?"

"A diner in Chicago."

On I-80 Somewhere in Iowa

After a several hours drive on I-80, Dave and his group were heading through Iowa toward Nebraska. Melinda was telling Dave about growing up in the future, meeting her late husband, and working with her children at the compound.

"Sounds like you've had a very interesting life," Dave said. "I think the most interesting thing I've ever done was to travel through Russia when I was younger."

Kendra listened closely to the music. "Excuse me, Dave. What is this music? I really like this one you're playing."

"This is the White Album by the Beatles, which is one of my all-time favorites."

"This is better than the music from our time," Kendra said.

"You don't have rock 'n' roll in the future?"

"Our music is more ambient. The Beatles are probably in our archives though," Melinda explained.

From a safe distance behind the van, the drone followed them.

Edwards Air Force Base
Area 51, Nevada

Kyle Clark watched the video feed of the van the drone was following. He was the UAS, Unmanned Aircraft Systems Operator, assigned to the base. Wayne stood behind him watching the video feed. He was reminded of the time he and his girlfriend had been glued to the television watching the police chase OJ Simpson's white Bronco.

"How long has he been on I-80?"

"Sir, for several hours."

"He's heading for Nevada," he said as he realized where the van could possibly be heading. "They're heading for this base."

"Sir?"

He stood there silently for several minutes thinking about all the reasons the time travelers could be heading their way. He rushed out of the Systems Operations Room and into the conference room. He walked up to the window and peered down at the J'onn 6. He remembered Malcolm mentioning the crashed spacecraft from Roswell could possibly possess time travel capabilities. He became concerned as he realized the danger they were in. He rushed out of the conference room and into Malcolm's office. "They're after the J'onn 6!"

"Are you certain?"

"The J'onn 6 is based off the technology of the Roswell spacecraft. Since it appears the van is heading our way, they could be planning to modify the J'onn 6 for time travel."

"We have a vast military presence here. There's no way they can get near the J'onn 6," Malcolm pointed out.

"Do we really want to take the risk?"

"What do you suggest?"

"We take them out. There's minimal traffic right now on I-80. A missile strike from the drone would do the trick," Wayne explained.

"If the public got word we killed US citizens with a drone on US soil…"

"We can claim they were a terrorist group planning an attack on Las Vegas."

Malcolm sat there quietly pondering the situation. "No, we want to capture them."

"Capture?"

"Think about all the technological advancements we can make with their knowledge of the future. Send one of our choppers with some of our best soldiers to intercept them before they reach Nevada."

"Right away."

Queen's Diner
Outside of Chicago

Rick and Marilyn sat at the counter of the Queen's Diner.

"Can I get you two something?" the heavyset, blonde waitress asked.

"Two coffees," Rick said.

She brought over two coffees and placed them in front of them. "So, who are you looking for?"

"How did you know we're looking for someone?" Marilyn asked.

"Your clothes. You are both wearing black suits. Business men don't normally eat in a dive like this. You are definitely FBI."

"Good observation," Rick said with a smile. "We were wondering if you saw this man. He was traveling with a couple of women." He placed his tablet on the counter which had Dave's BMV photo on it.

"Yes, I was working when they were here. They sat at the table in the far back away from everybody. Is he dangerous?"

"He's a person of interest," Rick answered. "Did you happen to hear any of their conversation?"

"When I brought over their food, they were talking about some machine. I didn't hear anything specific. He was with four people: two men and two women."

"Can you give us a description?" Marilyn asked.

"Even better. We have cameras." She pointed at the camera pointing toward the register and the one pointing toward the front door.

Rick looked over at Marilyn with a smile.

On I-80 Near The Nevada State Line

"I see the welcome to Nevada sign up ahead," Dave said.

As they drove closer to the Nevada state line, they could hear a humming noise getting louder. In the rearview mirror, Dave could see a large military transport chopper heading for them.

"We have company," Dave said.

The chopper flew past them. It was very low to the ground and turned around and landed in the middle of I-80 ahead of them. Soldiers climbed out of it and pointed their weapons toward their van. Dave slowed the van to a complete stop as the soldiers moved closer.

"Get out of your vehicle now with your hands up!" somebody said through the chopper's loudspeakers.

"Don't worry. I got this," Garth said as he slowly opened the door and got out.

The rest of them got out of the van as the soldiers drew closer. Garth walked a few steps away from the van toward the soldiers.

"Don't move another foot forward," one of the soldiers ordered.

"Memory wipe," Garth said as he pressed the button on the device that was in his pants pocket. The soldiers stood still in a state of complete confusion. They all dropped their weapons as their hands went completely numb. He pointed the device at the chopper disabling it.

"What did you do to them?" Dave asked, concerned.

"Don't worry. The effects are temporary. They won't remember what happened the past several hours. The paralysis will wear off in an hour or so. We better get out of here real quick." Garth spotted the drone as it moved closer. He pointed the device toward it and pressed the button. The drone crashed to the ground exploding on impact.

"As soon as we can, I suggest ditching this vehicle," Jepkins said.

"Go to the first town we see and we'll find something there," Garth ordered.

Edwards Air Force Base
Area 51, Nevada

Malcom and Wayne stood stunned after watching the events on I-80 take place through the drone's camera.

"What sort of weapons do they possess?" Malcolm pondered.

"Sir, I lost control of the drone!" Kyle shouted.

The screen went blank as the drone crashed.

"Contact Sergeant Whittaker!" Malcom ordered.

Wayne tried contacting the chopper, but no response. He looked over at Malcom who also looked worried.

"An EMP?" Malcom asked.

"Whatever it was also took out our soldiers, as well."

"We need to come up with some sort of plan," Malcom said. "We can't just let them barge in here and steal the J'onn 6."

"What do we possess that can stop technology from the future?" Wayne asked.

"I don't know."

Malcolm grabbed his cell phone out of his pocket and called Agent Venable. "I'm sending you a video of what just transpired on I-80. I need you to get there ASAP."

Oasis, Nevada

Dave stared at his van for the last time as Garth started the black 2015 Dodge Grand Caravan sitting in the driveway of one of the few houses in the small town. He pulled out of the driveway and drove away before the owner realized the vehicle was being stolen.

"I calculated a new route for us to follow. I suggest staying off of I-80. They probably will be looking for us on there," Jepkins instructed.

"I'm going to miss my van," Dave said sadly. "It was my mom's. She passed away from a heart attack a few months after purchasing it."

Melinda grasped his hands. "I know how it feels to lose a loved one. Everything left of my husband's possessions were on the compound. I'm not sure I'll ever see any of it again. As long as I keep his memory in my heart, he'll never be forgotten."

"I have plenty of great memories of my mother," he said reflecting back on all the good times.

Melinda kissed his right cheek.

"Thanks." David said blushing. He stared at the van for one last time as they drove away.

On I-80 near The Nevada State Line

Sergeant Whittaker felt a tingling sensation throughout his body as the paralysis began to wear off. He tried to remember the events that transpired on I-80 recently, but the last thing he could remember was eating a bowl of maple cinnamon oatmeal for breakfast. He tried calling the base, but none of the equipment in the chopper was operational. He could see a black helicopter heading in his direction. He slowly climbed out of the chopper. The soldiers were talking among themselves trying to figure out what had just transpired. None of them could remember anything.

The helicopter landed and Agent Venable walked over to him. "My name is Agent Rick Venable."

"None of us can remember what happened?"

"Maybe this video will refresh your memory."

Sergeant Whittaker watched the video in amazement. Even though he was watching what had happened, he still had no recollection of being a part of it. He looked at the soldiers and then back at Agent Venable. "I have no memory of this."

"They're heading for the base. We must stop them before they get there. We'll send a transport to pick up you and your men." Agent Venable walked away and a few seconds later the black helicopter took off.

"Their short term memories were erased," Rick said as he talked to Malcolm on the phone.

"Any ideas?" Malcolm asked.

"They most likely ditched the van by now. Does Dave Alexander have a cell phone or a laptop we can track?"

"Wayne is checking now. Yes, he has a tablet and it is active."

"We'll be able to track him."

"Sir, what about the device he used? Won't we be vulnerable to it, as well?" Marilyn asked, concerned.

"We'll have no choice but to wait for them to make their move on the base. We'll have to catch them off guard." Rick answered.

Edwards Air Force Base
Area 51, Nevada

Malcom and Wayne stood next to the J'onn 6 waiting for Mason Parsons to finish disabling it. He opened the hatch and climbed down the side.

"It's done. I disconnected the computer mainframe. It's not going anywhere without this." He showed them a small component about the size of a thumb drive.

"Now what?" Wayne asked.

"We find a way of defending ourselves from that weapon of theirs. If we could learn how to replicate their technology, we would possess the perfect weapon to defend this country from future terrorist attacks," Malcom answered.

"And make a fortune in the process," Wayne added.

"Of course," Malcolm said with a greedy smile.

Mason stared at Malcolm suspiciously. He didn't get assigned to Area 51 to develop weaponry. He was only interested in technological advancements to better mankind, not destroy it. He looked at the J'onn 6. Space exploration was the future.

"If we possessed their time traveling technology, we could go back in time and rewrite history for the good. Stop terrorist attacks before they happen. Imagine the possibilities," Malcolm said, his greedy smile getting bigger.

Mason stared at him. He pondered the dangers Malcolm could cause with that type of technology. He would have to be stopped. He looked back toward the J'onn 6. He would have to devise a plan for when the time travelers were captured.

"Mason, is there something wrong?" Wayne asked.

"No, just imagining the possibilities," Mason said and walked out of the hangar.

Groom Lake Road

"Restricted area. No trespassing beyond this point," Dave read as he stood in front of the sign on the road leading to Groom Lake where Area 51 was located near.

"We should be close enough for me to hack into the tranzer's computer," Garth said as he hacked into the base's computer via the tablet. He looked confused.

"What's wrong?" Melinda asked.

"I can't access its systems."

"They must have prepared for this," Jepkins said.

"Now what?" Kendra asked.

"We only have one option," Garth said sadly. "We must get captured."

"Captured? Are you crazy?" Dave looked at him angrily.

"If we can get inside the base, we can get to the tranzer."

"Insanity." Dave leaned against the sign, shaking his head in disbelief. "Do you have a plan?"

"First, we let them take us," Garth said as a black helicopter landed on the road behind them.

"I guess we aren't left with a choice," Dave said. "I hope it's a good plan."

Edwards Air Force Base
Area 51, Nevada

"Agent Venable has them," Malcolm said excitedly.

"They didn't put up a fight?" Wayne questioned.

"Not at all. They must have realized they were beaten after we disabled the J'onn 6."

"Seems too easy."

"Wayne, don't worry. We'll keep a security detail on them. We'll take all the necessary precautions with our guests."

"Our guests?"

"I'll try to extract their knowledge politely at first. If that doesn't work, I'll resort to using drastic measures."

"And their weapon they used on I-80?"

"Agent Venable has it in his possession. You can relax. Everything is under control."

"Malcolm, I sure hope so."

Mason opened the door leading to the vault containing the crashed spacecraft from Roswell. All the lights in the vault came on as he entered the hallway. He walked over to the spacecraft and admired its design. The J'onn 6 was almost an exact replica of it. For several years, he studied it learning everything he could about its technology in order to design the J'onn 6. Several of the systems on the crashed spacecraft were beyond repair. He suspected the system used for time travel was also destroyed in the crash.

He walked over to the glass casing which housed the metallic uniform the pilot was wearing and a small flat device damaged in the crash.

"Something bothering you?"

Mason turned around to acknowledge Russell White. "Just thinking."

"I've always wanted to take this one out for a test flight." Russell put his left hand on the spacecraft. "Knowing it can travel through time, I want to pilot it even more."

"If Malcolm has his way, you may get your chance."

"That bothers you?"

"Yes, it does. Nobody should possess the technology to go back in time and change history."

"Apparently somebody already possesses it. We are standing in front of the proof," Russell said as he stood next to Mason. "In a few minutes, we will get the honor of meeting real time travelers."

"I do have a lot of questions for them."

"And they will have a lot of answers. Come on, let's go meet them."

Malcom and Wayne watched as Agent Venable, with a security detail, led the travelers toward them.

"Agent Venable," Malcom acknowledged.

"Malcolm, it's been awhile. I don't believe you've met my associate, Agent Marilyn Austin."

Malcom shook her hand.

Agent Venable continued the introductions. "I want you to meet Melinda, Kendra, Garth, Jepkins and Dave."

"Welcome to Area 51. My name is Malcom Teller and this is Wayne Harris. If you'll follow us." Malcom led the group to the conference room. "We are eager to hear about how you arrived here."

Melinda told the tale of the compound and time traveling to 2015. While she told the story, Garth glanced down at the J'onn 6 in the hangar below.

As she finished the story, Malcom addressed Garth. "I see you are eyeing the J'onn 6."

"It's a beautiful ship," Garth responded.

"Yes, it is. I'm assuming you know a lot about it." Garth nodded.

"We are going to be launching it on its first mission soon. I'm assuming it will be a successful mission."

Garth nodded.

"I'm glad to hear it," Malcom said with a smile.

"I would love a tour of this facility," Garth said.

Wayne looked at Malcolm concerned.

"In due time. I propose an exchange of knowledge. There's a lot about your technology we are interested in learning about."

"You want to know how we can travel through time," Melinda said. "You can understand why it would be unwise for us to divulge that information. Any knowledge you learn from us can alter our timeline."

"Your timeline was altered the moment you traveled back in time," Wayne pointed out.

"He's right. If you were to travel back to the future, would it be as you left it," Malcolm added.

Garth looked over at Melinda. He never thought about what the ramifications to the timeline were from them traveling to the past. The future they knew may not even exist anymore.

"Whether you give us the information or not is your choice. I'm only asking if you would meet with our scientist and answer some of his questions. It could be beneficial to all of us."

"No promises, but we'll meet with him," Garth said. He needed to buy some time to devise a new plan to get him access to the J'onn 6. Until then, he would play along with Malcolm's curiosity.

Malcolm and Wayne stood up. "We'll send our scientist in to speak with you. Agent Venable, I'd like to speak to you in private."

Malcom and Wayne walked out of the room followed by Rick and Marilyn.

"Let me see the weapon they used on I-80," Malcom requested.

"This way."

He led them to the desk in Malcolm's office where a black metallic case was sitting. Malcolm opened it and his eyes widened as he saw the device. It looked similar to the one in the glass casing in the vault.

"You've seen this before?" Rick asked.

"Yes, we have it here. Our scientists could never get it to work due to how damaged it was. Modified on a greater scale, this weapon could disable all our enemies."

"And make us billionaires," Wayne added.

"Billionaires," he repeated with a big smile.

Mason and Russell walked into the conference room.

"Mason!" Melinda, Kendra, Garth and Jepkins said in shock.

"You guys all know me?"

"Yes, you are the leading scientist at our compound," Melinda answered.

"From the future?"

"You two were aboard the tranzer when it traveled to our time," Garth answered.

"You guys are the first time travelers," Jepkins added.

"You can help us," Melinda said.

"How?"

"By helping us get to the tranzer, the J'onn 6, and pilot us to the ripple in the space time continuum," Garth answered.

"You want us to take you to the future?" Russell asked, excited.

"You did it before. This time, we will accompany you," Kendra said.

Mason looked at Russell. The idea of traveling to the future sounded exciting and being a scientist, he couldn't pass up the opportunity. "You have a plan how we can get to the J'onn 6 without Malcolm stopping us?"

"Yes, I do. I need the device Agent Venable took from us," Garth answered. "With it, we can paralyze everyone here long enough to escape in the J'onn 6 and wipe the memory of everyone here so there is no recollection of the past few hours."

"We would have to erase all the files on you guys and the events of today from the base's computers. They will wonder what happened to the J'onn 6 when they recover from the device's effects," Jepkins added.

"Are you with us?" Melinda asked.

Mason looked at Russell who nodded in agreement. "Yes, we're in."

Mason walked into Malcolm's office where Malcolm and Wayne were admiring the device.

"Did you learn anything useful from them?" Malcolm asked.

"Yes, I did. I have an idea how to modify the J'onn 6 for time travel. They are explaining to Russell how to find the ripple in the space time continuum. I want to take the device to my lab and run some tests."

"Take it." Malcolm handed it to him. "The sooner you can learn its secrets, the sooner we can replicate its technology."

"Too bad, in a moment, you won't remember its existence." He pressed the button on the device's side.

"What…" Malcolm began to say as his short-term memory was being altered.

Malcolm and Wayne stared at him emotionlessly as they were being paralyzed by the effects.

Mason walked out of the office and handed the device to Garth. "I'll head to the Systems Room and erase all the data relating to you guys. I will rendezvous with you at the J'onn 6. Reinstall this back into its computer mainframe." He handed Garth the component he uninstalled earlier.

"Mason, thanks," Garth said as they split up.

Mason ran for the Systems Room. He entered it and walked over to the main computer. He sat down and began deleting everything about the travelers on file.

"What are you doing?" Agent Venable asked as he walked into the room. "I just found Malcolm and Wayne in a zombie-like state. You're helping them escape." He had his gun pointed at Mason. "You're not going to get away with this."

"I'm doing this for our own good."

"Are you?"

"We, in this current timeframe, are not ready for time travel. It can only lead to disaster."

"That's not your decision to make," Rick said as he walked over to the computer.

"Do you really want this technology to fall into the wrong hands?"

Rick lowered his weapon as he thought about the consequences of the government in control of time-travel. He thought about all the history he had read in school and how in one instance, somebody could completely change the course of history for their benefit. He knew Mason was right and he decided it was in everybody's best interest to help him.

"No, I don't. Did you erase everything?"

"Yes."

"Good. Now get them out of here."

Mason looked at him puzzled.

"Mason, I've seen things over the years the normal person can't comprehend. I'm a strong believer in the greater good. Nothing good can come out of us being able to travel through time. Get the J'onn 6 out of here. I'm going to destroy everything in the vault. Now that I know what the ship in there is capable of, I know what a real threat it poses."

"Thanks."

"Mason, good luck," Rick said and shook his hand.

"The J'onn 6 is fully operational. I'm plotting its course," Garth reported.

"I've looked over your data. I should be able to navigate us through the ripple in space," Russell assured him.

Outside the J'onn 6, Melinda and Dave waited for Mason.

"I'm going to miss this place. Not Area 51. I mean 2015," Dave said.

"You're going to love the future."

Mason ran into the hangar. "It's been taken care of."

"Shall we," Melinda said as she climbed the ladder leading to the hatch on the top of the J'onn 6.

As everybody sat down, Garth gave the order to take off. The J'onn 6 flew out of the hangar and headed for space.

"To the future," Melinda said.

"To the future," everybody repeated in unison.

The Compound, 2684

"They are breaking through are defenses!" Jepkins reported.

"The tranzer's ready," Marty reported.

"I'm ready," Garth said as the tranzer spun faster producing a large gateway.

The door to the compound burst open. Garth jumped through the gateway followed by Kendra and Jepkins.

"Melinda, go now," Marty yelled as he was shot in the chest by a laser blast.

"Marty!"

A tall muscular man in red metallic armor pointed his laser rifle at her. She jumped through the gateway before he could fire the blast.

Before the man could jump through the gateway after her, he was shot in the chest. A group of soldiers led by Garth and Jepkins rushed into the compound and shot all of the invading soldiers. As the enemy was defeated, Melinda and Dave walked into the room behind them. Melinda ran over to Marty.

"You made it back," Marty said.

"Don't move" she said as their doctor tended to his wound.

"Who is this?" Marty asked, looking at Dave.

"This is Dave, my husband."

"Husband?" Marty asked.

"It's a long story," Melinda said and told him the story about going back to 2015 and returning to 2068 months before the events that just transpired in the compound. "We didn't know who the enemy was so we had to wait for them to attack the compound. During that time, Dave and I fell in love. Now we are back in time, meeting for the first time and falling in love all over again."

"Now that's a time loop worth being stuck in," Dave said and kissed Melinda.

"Agreed," Melinda said with a smile.

Musings From Derek's Mind

BUZZ KILL

"Julianne, I need you to take these garbage bags to the dumpster out back," Antonia Martinez, the grocery manager of Super Savings grocery store, ordered.

Julianne gave her a dirty look as she walked away from the sink in the backroom where she had just dumped a bucket of dirty mop water. She was very short with long blonde hair with orange highlights. With her tiny frame and fair pale skin, she was constantly hit on by customers and her co-workers. She didn't mind, because she loved all the attention. It helped with her low self-esteem. She walked over to Antonia and grabbed the two garbage bags. She walked out the receiving door without acknowledging her.

She walked down the concrete ramp leading to the dumpster. A guy was standing in front of the dumpster digging through the garbage looking for food he could salvage.

"Can I help you?" Julianne asked.

"I think I found what I needed," the man said, never looking at her. "I was just leaving." He got in his truck and drove away.

"Damn freegans," she said as she threw one of the garbage bags into the dumpster. A bee flew out of the dumpster causing her to run backward in fear. It chased her for a second and then flew away in the opposite direction. Her heart beat fast with fear. She was allergic to bees and normally she would carefully throw the bags into the dumpster without incident. She cautiously walked back to the dumpster and threw the second bag in. When she was finished, she walked back through the receiving doors.

"Are you ok?" Marlena, the receiving clerk, asked. "You are breathing heavily."

"Yes, I just had an encounter with an angry bee."

"If you don't bother them, they won't bother you."

"That is just a myth," Julianne said angrily as she walked past her.

Jason, the stocker working in the organic section, waived at her as she walked out onto the sales floor. She walked over to him. "Hey, slacker!"

"Me? A slacker? I never see you stock anything."

"That's because I'm a bagger."

"Definition of bagger: one who stands around and does nothing all day," he joked.

"And gets paid the same as you," she said, laughing as she walked away.

Jason watched her walk away. She was the most beautiful girl he'd ever seen. He was obsessed with her. All the walls in his room were filled with posters he made of her from pictures he downloaded off of her Facebook page. He spent every night dreaming what his life would be like if she was his wife. He had a sinister smile on his face as he fantasized making love to her in the back of his red minivan. One way or the other, she would be his; willingly or unwillingly.

Julianne walked over to the dairy department and faced all the product on the shelves making the department appear to be full. As she heard her name on the intercom, she walked to the front to bag some groceries.

"Julianne, Jason's staring at you again," Roberta, the cashier for the register she was bagging at, warned.

"Him, he's harmless as a kitten."

"I think he's creepy. With his hairstyle and the way he walks and talks, he reminds me of Norman Bates."

"More like Napoleon Dynamite," Julianne laughed.

"Girls, we're here to work, not chit chat. We don't have conversations like this in front of customers," Deana, the front manager, warned.

"Sorry," Julianne said to the customer waiting in line.

"It's ok. I thought it was amusing," the elderly lady, buying a lot of Fancy Feast, said.

George Thomas watched as the dock loaders of Kellville Bees filled the back of his open semi-truck with boxes of over four hundred bee hives. He was going to transport millions of bees to Mason's Blueberry Farm. It was taking them longer to carefully fill the truck with the hives. If he was going to get the delivery to its destination on time, he would have to drive a little faster than normal when he got on the interstate. He hoped the traffic wasn't going to be backed up due to the construction they were doing on the left lanes on the interstate.

"We're almost done," one of the loaders assured him.

"It's about time," he said impatiently.

"Be careful transporting them," the loader warned.

"I will."

After eight long hours of bagging groceries and facing up all the aisles, Julianne's shift was over. She was exhausted. Except for the two fifteen minute breaks, she was on her feet the whole time. She wanted to get home and take a long soothing bath. As she was walking out the store, she spotted Jason standing nervously by her car. *Was he going to ask her out?* She went over all the reasons why she couldn't go out with him and decided which reason she would kindly give him. She didn't want to date him, but she also didn't want to hurt his feelings. After a minute of thinking, she walked over to her car.

"Julianne," he stuttered.

"What's up, slacker?"

"I was wondering if you would go out on a date with me." He was staring at her feet, never making eye contact with her as he asked. She felt nervous as he asked her out because the way he did it reminded her of Norman Bates.

"Jason, you're a nice guy and I like you as a friend."

"A friend?" He seemed very agitated by the word friend.

"Besides, I'm seeing this guy. He's a freshman in college." As she was speaking, she was fumbling for her keys in her purse.

"I see," he said sadly, still staring at her feet.

"I'm sorry," she said as she pressed the unlock button on her keypad. As she reached for the door, he grabbed the back of her head and slammed it into the driver's side window of her car. She fell to the ground unconscious.

"Get out of the fast lane, granny!" George yelled as he drove down the interstate. He could see the sign directing traffic to move to the right lane. The cars in front of him were slowly merging into the right lane almost causing a bottleneck ahead. The car in front of him stopped abruptly to avoid hitting the car ahead of it. He swerved to avoid a collision and forced the car to the right of him into the railing. He lost control and jackknifed his truck. As the cab of the truck hit the concrete barrier on the left, the trailer slammed into multiple cars spilling all the boxes containing the bee hives all over the interstate.

Blood was trickling down the side of George's face as he slowly climbed out of the cab. He was covered in bees and his skin was beginning to swell. He felt the bees stinging him. As he screamed, several bees instantly flew into his mouth stinging his tongue and the inside of his mouth.

As all the cars stopped to avoid the massive pileup building up ahead, they were being covered with bees. Those who unfortunately had their windows down or vents open were being swarmed by bees.

Julianne slowly opened her eyes. She had a massive headache and was having a hard time adjusting to the light. She tried to move her hands but she could barely move them. As her vision cleared, she could see her hands were handcuffed to an old wooden bedpost. To the right of her was a dirty window with a rotten frame. In front of her was a large metal door with a small wooden desk in front of it. The ground was concrete. She could barely lift her legs a few feet, because they were tied down with rope. To the right of the bed she could see light shining through a golf-ball sized hole in the middle of the wall which was rotted. She could smell motor oil. She was in someone's garage.

"Help!" she screamed.

No response.

After a few minutes of screaming, she gave up. The last thing she remembered was trying to get into her car after the awkward encounter with Jason. She looked around the room hoping to find something close she could free herself with. She was secured tightly. Even if there was something she could use, there was no way she could get to it. She tried listening, hoping to hear somebody outside the room, but the only thing she could hear was the humming from the fluorescent light above her.

She thought about all the horror films she watched over the years. None of them ever had a happy ending. She pictured all the graphic scenes from the Saw movies and began to cry. She tried to regain her composure. She didn't want to go into a panic attack while handcuffed to the bed. She looked down and realized she wasn't wearing the uniform from work. She was wearing a fancy red dress. Jason had undressed her and put her in the dress while she was unconscious. She tried not to imagine what else he did to her, but she had a vivid imagination.

"Stop it," she said, trying to erase the images from her mind. "You have to be strong. You can get out of this."

"This is Randy Pacini reporting from I-80/94. As you can see from the wreckage behind me, a truck carrying millions of bees jackknifed sending swarms of bees in every direction. I've been stung once and my camera man has been stung twenty times. We are now reporting from a safe distance. As you can see, bee keepers are trying to salvage as many of the hives as they can. They are urging people to stay away from I-80/94 and to those stuck in the traffic jam to keep their windows up and vents closed."

"Jason, that's not too far from our house. You should stay inside where it's safe."

"Mother, I have to go to work soon," Jason said as he brought his mother a cup of herbal tea.

"Did you put enough milk in here? I don't like it when it's bitter."

"I made it exactly the way you like it. You should turn the news off. It will only give you nightmares," Jason advised.

"I will after the weather report. Now give your mother a kiss before you go to work."

He kissed the side of her right cheek.

"You are such a good boy. You'll make some lucky woman a great husband."

"Thanks, mom."

Julianne tried sliding her tiny right hand out of the handcuffs with little luck. She heard a car door slam. A few seconds later, the door ahead opened and Jason walked in carrying an old, red plastic lunchbox. He walked over to the side of the bed and sat down on the metal chair next to it.

"I brought you some food. I know you're probably hungry."

"Can you take off the handcuffs? I promise to be a nice girl."

She was staring at him seductively.

"Nice try, Julianne. I'm not that gullible." He opened up the lunchbox and pulled out a small juice box. He put the straw in it and put it in front of her mouth. "Drink. I don't want you dying of thirst." She willingly sucked the juice through the straw. "Now I want you to eat."

"Why are you doing this?"

"So we can be together like a loving couple."

"It's not real."

"It is to me and that's all that matters."

"Don't you care about my well-being?"

"Julianne, be a good girl and I promise I won't hurt you. You're safe here." He offered her a peanut butter sandwich and she bit into it. "Small bites. I don't want you to choke."

After she had finished the whole sandwich and drank the rest of the juice box, Jason grabbed a book off of the wooden desk and sat down next to her. He read the book aloud to her for thirty minutes while she tried not to cry. He put the book on the desk and then kissed her on the top of her head.

"I have to go to work now. Unfortunately, I think one of their baggers will be a no show."

"They'll know I'm missing. My car's still in the parking lot."

"They'll never suspect me." He walked out of the garage. A few seconds later she heard his car drive away.

She wept for several minutes. She looked down and spotted a bee sitting on her dress. She tried staying completely still hoping it would fly away. She turned her head to the right and saw several bees crawling through the hole in the wall. She could feel something crawling on her head. She didn't know if her mind was playing tricks on her or if a bee was actually crawling through her hair. More bees crawled through the hole. Within minutes, the whole wall was covered in a swarm of bees. She watched in horror as hundreds of bees crawled through the hole. Within half an hour she was completely covered with them. She was paralyzed in fear. She could feel them crawling all over her face. She tried not to open her mouth. She could feel a tingling sensation in both her ears as they crawled inside. She could feel her skin swell from being stung. Within seconds she could no longer see through the bees covering her eyes. She was in complete agony from the pain from the swelling until she felt a complete numbness going through her body and then unconsciousness.

Jason parked his car in front of the garage of the abandoned house long forgotten in the woods near I-80/94. He and his friends discovered it when they were kids and used it as a hideout for several years. As he got out of his car, a bee landed on his arm. He looked at it. He never saw a bee out this late before. Normally at this time of night, they were inactive. He flicked it away with his finger and walked toward the garage. He walked in and dropped the bag of tacos in shock. Julianne was standing in front of him completely naked. The handcuffs were sitting on the bed ripped in half and the ropes looked completely chewed through.

"Julianne, how did you get free?"

"Jason, does it matter?" She walked over to him seductively. "Does this body turn you on?"

"Yes," he said, stuttering.

"You will do perfectly."

"Perfectly for what?"

"A new hive." She opened her mouth and a thousand bees flew out of it and straight into Jason's. He fell to the ground as the swarm completely engulfed him.

Julianne laughed as she watched Jason become a hive for the bees. "I have four hundred more hives to relocate."

She grabbed the keys from his pocket. She grabbed the red dress and put it back on and walked out of the garage. She got into his car and drove toward the exit ramp leading to I-80/94 where the rest of the bees were waiting for her to rescue them.

A Horror Story

"Everybody, I need your ideas on what the next great horror franchise will be," Art Kollins, the head of Tigerfence movie studios, said. He sat at the front of the conference table staring at the group of screenplay writers and production staff.

"How about a story about a ghost haunting an orphanage? Ninety minutes where nothing happens with a budget less than a million," Leo Maziky suggested.

"Brilliant. Sounds like a blockbuster in the making," Art said excitedly.

"Using lighting and sound effects, we wouldn't have to unveil what the ghost looks like until the last ten minutes," Leo continued.

"People will eat it up." Art wiped the saliva from the corner of his mouth. He loved what he was hearing.

"We can also have a cat jump out of a closet to put a cheap scare into the viewers," Helena Smith, another script writer, added.

"Audiences love cat scares," Leo agreed.

"And the plot?" Art asked.

"Doesn't need one. As long as we can every twenty minutes throw out a cheap scare, we have a hit," Helena said.

"Have scary looking dolls in the background in every scene. I love seeing those in the background. The camera man can occasionally do close-ups. They wouldn't be relevant to the story at all," Art said while everybody nodded in agreement. "Leo and Helena can quickly write the script while Tamara and Stephen can work on the set designs. Make it as eerie as possible."

Leo and Helena sat at the back table of the diner across from the movie studio throwing story ideas back and forth. Helena was reading from her tablet a story about a supposed haunted orphanage that had been abandoned since the fifties. Leo watched her closely as she read. She was the most beautiful woman he had ever met. Her long raven-black hair ran down past her shoulders. She was very short and petite. She was originally from Romania, but moved to California with her parents when she was a teenager. He had been in love with her for years, but their relationship never moved past the friendship stage.

"Leo, the orphanage is only a five hour drive from here. Let's spend the night there."

"In a haunted orphanage?"

"Yes, imagine how authentic our script will be if we stay there. If we're lucky, we may encounter a ghost."

"Don't you mean unlucky?"

"Maybe Stephen and Tamara will want to join us."

Before he could say anything, she was on her phone talking to Tamara. "Cool. Meet us at the diner."

"I take it they're on board."

She nodded.

"We'll need to pick up some flashlights."

"And candles. To get us in the horror mood," she said with a smile.

"Let me guess – Ouija board."

"No, silly. That's been done to death," Helena said with a smile. She always smiled at his sarcastic remarks.

"Clichés are the best part of a horror film. The fans are expecting the norm."

"Don't you want to be original? Write a script you can be proud of?"

"I guess I can conjure up a great idea."

She raised her left eyebrow at him. "Conjure? Resorting to horror puns now?"

"This whole project is going to be one big pun," he said, trying not to yawn.

"Not if we put our heart," she waited a few seconds before continuing, "and soul into it."

The door to the diner opened and Stephen and Tamara walked in. Tamara had her blonde hair tied in a bun and wore a t-shirt from her favorite zombie television series. Stephen was wearing camping gear and carried a large duffle bag.

"Stephen, we are only spending the night," Helena said.

"I brought plenty of munchies. I'm also prepared for any dangers." He unzipped the duffel bag exposing a rifle.

"Expecting a ghost of a killer deer?" Leo asked.

"You never know what may be lurking around there," Stephen said in a deep scary voice.

"We better get going while there is still daylight left," Tamara advised.

"I just checked my weather app. There are thunderstorms in the forecast," Helena said.

"Mother Nature, bring it on!" Leo shouted as he exited the diner.

"Yep, he'll be the first to die," Tamara chuckled.

The group debated what was the greatest horror film of all time during the five hour drive. Each one of them had their favorite pick and did their best to try to prove it to each other. They drove off the main road and followed a narrow dirt road leading to the orphanage. The road led them through a wooded area that appeared to have been undisturbed for a long time. The sky was darkening as it was filled with storm clouds. Leo slammed on his breaks to avoid hitting a deer that jumped out from the trees to the right.

"Leo, are you all right?" Helena asked as she watched him trying to regain his composure.

"It came out of nowhere."

"Leo, maybe it was the killer ghost deer."

"Stephen, that's not funny," Tamara said as she punched his arm.

"Are we going to continue or are you too scared now?" Helena asked.

"I'm fine," he said and drove forward.

A mile up the road they could see the orphanage. It was a large building all boarded up. The grass was almost five feet tall, being neglected for many years, making it hard for them to see the orphanage from the road. As they drew closer, they could see an old playground with what was left standing of a swing set and a slide. They pulled into the dirt driveway leading to the front of the orphanage. As they exited the vehicle, they were hit by the stench of decay. They couldn't figure out what was causing the smell, but it was the worst thing either of them had ever smelled in their life.

"Check to see if there is any tools in the trunk. The front door is boarded up," Helena said.

"Helena, judging by the look of the wood, it will probably crumble in our hands," Leo said as he touched the wood. Stephen brought over a hammer and Leo used it to pry off the wood nailed to the front door. After a couple of minutes, he had them all removed.

"Who wants to go first?" Stephen asked. He waited a few minutes for someone to volunteer. "Fine, I'll go first." He grabbed the rusted door knob and pulled on the door. At first it didn't want to budge, but then he was able to slowly open it. It made a loud screeching sound as it hadn't been opened in decades. They were instantly hit with a sour smell worse than the one they were smelling outside.

Leo shined his flashlight into the foyer. Inside was a long corridor with hallways leading to the left and the right. There was a large staircase toward the back next to a door marked admittance office. There was a tall statue adjacent to the staircase. As he shined the flashlight on the floor, mice scattered in every direction.

"Forget designing sets. This place is perfect for filming a movie," Stephen said excitedly. "And this is just the foyer. Imagine what the rest of the place looks like. I wonder what's upstairs."

"Let's investigate down here first before venturing upward. Be careful. We don't know what the condition of this place might be. The steps on the staircase could be rotted through as well as the upstairs flooring. We don't want one of us accidentally falling to our deaths," Leo warned.

Helena and Tamara both jumped as they heard the loud sound of thunder outside. The front door slammed violently behind them. They all jumped backward.

"The wind?" Tamara asked

"Probably from the storm," Stephen suggested.

Helena pulled out her smart phone to check the weather forecast, but she couldn't connect to the internet.

"We are in the middle of nowhere. I doubt there is any signal out here," Leo said.

They followed the hallway to the right which led to what used to be the dining room. There were scratches on the floor where the dining table and chairs once stood. The room brightened briefly from the flash of lightning outside.

"This is going to be a long night," Tamara said nervously.

"But a fun one," Stephen said, nudging her.

"Stephen, stop it."

"I'm assuming the kitchen is this way," Helena guessed as she pushed the swinging door forward which fell off its hinges and landed on the floor. "Time hasn't been good to this place."

The window behind them burst inward as a large branch from the tree outside crashed through. They could hear the roar of a tornado nearby.

"I hope it's not heading in our direction." Leo walked over to the window and looked out. "I can see it in the distance. It looks massive."

Helena walked over to him and looked for herself. "I don't think this place could withstand somebody outside sneezing on it. It looks like it's heading in the opposite direction."

"Can we resume the tour?" Stephen asked.

"Until the severe storm passes we should stay on the lower level," Leo suggested, moving away from the window.

They continued through the kitchen and back down the hallway to the foyer. Leo shined his flashlight upward toward a large chandelier covered in spider webs. "I didn't notice that when we entered. It could be worth a fortune."

"What about the statue over there?" Stephen shined his flashlight at the statue's head. It depicted an elderly man with a mustache and a monocle on his left eye. The name plate on the bottom of the statue read: Lord William

Acland. He looked back up and jumped back when he thought the statue's eyes had moved.

"Getting jittery?" Tamara asked, nudging him.

"His eyes moved."

"It's just your mind playing tricks on you. You're in a haunted house," Leo reminded him.

"Just my mind playing tricks," he repeated to himself.

"Let's see where the hallway to the left leads," Leo suggested.

The group followed him down the hallway into a large room filled with empty bookshelves. They could hear the sound of heavy rain falling from outside with continuous loud thunder. The room instantly went dark as all four of their flashlights went out. Tamara screamed as she felt something large brush against her leg.

"Tamara!" Stephen tried to feel his way toward her in the pitch dark. "I can't find you."

"I'm over here," she cried.

Leo repeatedly pressed the button on his flashlight. "I think the battery is dead."

"How can all of our flashlight batteries go dead at the same time?" Helena asked.

"Not sure." Leo answered.

Tamara jumped as Stephen put his hand on her shoulder. "It's just me."

"I'm starting to think this was a bad idea," Tamara said, trying not to go into a panic attack.

All of their flashlights suddenly came back on. In the corner of the room was a large raccoon staring at them. It ran away as Leo shined his flashlight at it.

"At least it wasn't a cat," Stephen said.

"Not funny," Tamara said softly.

Stephen could tell she was becoming annoyed with him. "Sorry, that was insensitive. I'm sort of scared myself."

"You have a funny way of showing it." She punched him in the shoulder signifying she was all right.

"All of our flashlights went off and back on at the same time. It's too area 51ish," Helena said puzzled.

"Guys, we're here for inspiration for a horror movie not a sci-fi one," Stephen pointed out.

"Why can't it be a little of both?" Leo asked.

"Budgetary reasons. Good horror movies can be done with little or no money. Sci-fi can't."

"Stephen has a point," Helena said.

"The rain has stopped. I can see the moon poking out behind the storm clouds," Leo said as he stared out the window. "I think it may be safe enough to venture upstairs now."

"You first."

"Wow, Stephen. Maybe you are a little bit scared," Tamara teased.

"No. He's older and wiser than us which makes him a natural born leader."

"Keep rationalizing and maybe you will be convinced you're brave." Tamara nudged him forward. They all followed behind Leo in a single file.

They slowly walked up the stairs each step squeaking under their feet. The more steps they climbed, the worse the smell was getting. Tamara had to stop herself from throwing up all over Stephen's back. They reached the second floor and there were six doors along the hallway. Leo opened the first one on the left. Inside the room were six beds along with a large book case filled with a vast doll collection covered in dust and spider webs. He touched one of the dolls and its brittle dress crumbled in his hand. He shined his flashlight on the dolls and felt a shiver run down his spine as he realized all the dolls were missing their eyes.

"Now that's creepy," Helena said, inspecting the dolls closely. "Who would do that to them?"

"Maybe it happened over time from being neglected in this place." Leo shined his flashlight toward the beds. All the mattresses were ripped apart probably from all the mice they had been seeing throughout the place.

"Still, it's creepy looking. I'm getting a lot of ideas for a great script," Helena said with a smile.

Tamara dropped her flashlight when she heard the screams from what sounded like a little child.

"Sounds like it's coming from across the hall," Leo said.

"We're the only ones here, right?" Tamara asked.

The screams were getting louder and now it sounded like a whole group of children were screaming. They could also hear what sounded like a whip being cracked repeatedly as the screams continued.

"Somebody's being tortured!" Tamara shouted frantically.

The screams suddenly stopped, and they heard loud footprints heading toward them. A large glowing green specter slowly floated into the room and stared at them with glowing red eyes. It tightly held a large whip in its hands. It opened its mouth wide, and they could hear the loud screaming again emanating from it. It closed its mouth and the screaming stopped. It cracked the whip toward them causing them to jump backward. Satisfied they were afraid of it, it floated out of the room. Again they heard the sounds of the screaming children and the whip cracking repeatedly.

"That's our cue to leave," Leo said.

Stephen put his duffel bag on the ground and grabbed the shotgun. "Just in case."

They slowly crept down the stairway to avoid alerting the specter. The foyer was filled with several specters of children being led down the left hallway by a female specter wearing clothing which looked like they were from the Civil War era. The living room was filled with vintage furniture. A specter which looked similar to the statue of Lord William Acland stood by the front door holding a Springfield rifle shouting: "Damn Confederates!"

"I'm confused. What's a Lord doing in the States during the Civil War?" Stephen asked.

"We are surrounded by ghosts and that's what you're wondering," Leo whispered.

The orphanage shook slightly as they heard what sounded like cannon fire.

"Civil War reenactment of the dead?" Helena asked.

"Whatever it is, we are trapped," Leo answered.

"You there on the stairs, drop your weapon at once! The element of surprise is not on your side!" Lord Acland ordered, pointing his rifle toward them.

Stephen quickly dropped the rifle onto the floor at the end of the stairs.

"Samuel, pull yourself away from beating the slave folk and come down here immediately! We have intruders!" Lord Acland shouted.

The specter holding the whip slowly made its way down the staircase. They slowly walked downward as it stared at them. It forced them toward Lord Acland.

"Don't expect much talk from Samuel. His tongue was removed during the war for disobeying a direct order of mine. Are you Union or Confederate?"

"I'm an American," Stephen answered.

Lord Acland grabbed him by the neck. "You have a strong neck. It really doesn't matter. They all snap the same hanging from a noose. Samuel, prepare them for a quadruple hanging."

Samuel smiled as he forced them forward. Lord Acland opened the door and they were forced out the door by Samuel. As they walked through the door, they stood in shock as they were in the foyer of the orphanage again. The specters were gone and the living room was empty.

"What just happened?" Helena asked.

"Not sure." Leo shined his flashlight toward the stairs, and Stephen's rifle was laying where he had dropped it. He walked over to the rifle and examined it. The metal plating was rusted and it was covered in layers of dust.

"It looks old. How long has it been sitting here?" Stephen asked.

"This doesn't make any sense," Tamara said.

"Did we just travel through time?" Helena asked.

"We need to get out of here immediately." Leo led them out the front door and on the other side of it was the foyer of the orphanage again.

Stephen looked at Leo confused. They turned around and walked out the door and into the foyer on the other side.

"We can't leave!" Tamara screamed.

They could hear screaming coming from above. This time the sounds were from a woman followed by the sound of a chainsaw. The screams got louder as the sound of the chainsaw continued. They felt their feet getting wetter. They looked down and they were standing in a pool of blood. Tamara ran for the front door.

"Tamara, wait!" Stephen screamed.

She ran out the front door and into the room full of dolls upstairs. She was shaking violently with fear. The sun was shining through the window, and she could see the dolls staring at her with their eyeless faces.

"Play with me!" Their mouths moved in unison as they continued to shout, "Play with me!"

She screamed and ran out of the room crashing into a large man dressed in an executioner's outfit. He grabbed her by the arm and dragged her down the stairs where a guillotine was waiting for her. A man wearing a priest outfit from biblical times held a large parchment.

"Tamara Largent, you are charged with performing witchcraft and are sentenced to death by beheading."

The executioner forced her into the guillotine. A black cat walked over to her and began licking her face. The priest motioned to the executioner and seconds later the blade came down severing her head from her body.

Helena screamed as Tamara's head rolled down the stairs before them. The pool of blood was rising fast. If they didn't get out of the foyer quickly, they would drown in the blood.

"Swim toward the stairs!" Leo ordered.

They swam toward the stairs and quickly ran up them. They turned to the right and ran into a Roman arena from the gladiator days.

A large muscular gladiator covered in battle scars approached them holding a large ax. "Choose your weapons! We fight to the death!"

"We aren't warriors!" Helena screamed.

"If you are not warriors, then you are cowards! Cowards must die! Women have no place in an arena!" The gladiator pushed Helena into the passageway where they entered. She emerged back into the room filled with the dolls.

"Play with me!" Their mouths moved in unison as they continued to shout, "You're the one who gets to play with me!" One of them jumped onto the floor, and then each one in turn jumped onto the previous one until they formed one gigantic doll. "I will play with you like little Cindy played with me!" It pushed her hard against one of the bedposts. She screamed as it jumped on top of her and pressed its fingers into her eyes pushing them way back into her skull. She continued to scream until her life was squeezed out of her body from the strength of the doll's hands.

Leo and Stephen stood their ground as the gladiator swung his ax toward them. Leo deflected the blow with his shield sending him backward. A crack formed on it from the impact.

"Puny little boy! One more blow from my ax and you're dead!" the gladiator shouted as the crowd cheered, "I bring you another victory!"

"Head for the passageway. It should lead us out of here," Leo ordered. He stood up and slowly backed away toward the passageway.

Stephen slowly moved over to Leo as he moved toward the passageway. Leo, making sure Stephen was close enough, walked through the passageway. Stephen was almost to the passageway when he felt a sharp pain. He looked down and a large sphere was sticking out of his chest. The last thing he heard before he died was the gladiator chanting, "Another victory!"

Leo was standing alone in the middle of the foyer of the orphanage. A tall beautiful redhead was standing before him. She wore a white see-through cloak. She walked up to him seductively.

"Such a pretty specimen. Do you like what you see? All men like what they see when they are in my presence. I'm very hungry and you look like the perfect specimen to feed my hunger." She licked his neck. He could hear a loud hissing sound from behind him. He turned around just in time to see the large python's head come down and swallow him whole.

"Don't be in such a rush," Julie said as she helped Jermaine remove the camera equipment out of the back of his van.

"This place will be perfect for the next episode of Haunted America. Kevin, make sure there is a camera set up in each room," Jermaine said.

The five members of Jermaine's crew grabbed the remaining cameras and headed for the orphanage's front door.

From the window the specter of Lord Acland watched them. "Damn Confederates!"

Lumps of Coal

Mitt Vanderbilt sat admiring his blanket made out of hundred dollar bills. He couldn't get a peaceful night's sleep without money touching his bare skin. Hanging on the walls surrounding him were paintings from around the world appraised to be worth millions of dollars. He climbed out of bed and walked into his bathroom which was the size of a typical person's whole apartment. He admired himself in the mirror. He was a tall, handsome man with a defined chin. Anybody could tell from his distinguished appearance he was made of money. He was the president of a multi-billion dollar corporation that made its money on the backs of minimum wage workers – his slaves as he referred to them. He didn't feel guilty for making his money off of the unfortunate. As he told his business partners: the reason people worked for minimum wage was because they were lazy.

"You are a powerful man. Now go make some more billions," he said to his reflection.

He walked into the main room of his mansion while watching the daily business report on his smartphone. His maid, Rosita, was vacuuming. He ignored her as he walked into the dining room. He sat down at the table as his kitchen staff prepared his breakfast. His butler, Jared, poured him a cup of Kopi luwak, one of the most expensive coffees in the world. He never looked up to acknowledge them as he watched the report on the smartphone. He never paid any attention to his servants.

After getting dressed for another day at the corporate office, he walked outside where his limo driver was standing, waiting for his arrival.

"Good day, sir. To the office?"

Mitt nodded his head as he sat down on the backseat.

While driving through the city, Mitt glanced up briefly and noticed a long line of people bundled up in cheap coats outside of a church.

"What's going on over there?"

"It's the food bank. It's the Tuesday before Christmas."

"Damn takers! If it wasn't for that damn forty-seven percent, I wouldn't have to pay so much in taxes! Why are people starving? I'll tell you the answer! They are too lazy to get a real job!"

"Yes, sir."

Mitt sat at the conference table at the corporate office listening to the board members discussing the plans for making more billions in 2015. He sat there salivating at the thought his net worth would increase again next year. The more money he possessed, the happier he was. After the meeting was over, he headed for his favorite Five-Star restaurant. As he exited his limo, a homeless lady walked over to him.

"Sir, can you spare a couple of dollars so I can get something to eat."

"Get away from me. I don't give money away to peasants."

"I lost my job. I'm forced to live on the streets."

"Not my problem. Any intelligent person would have gotten another job. It's not that difficult. Now get out of my way. I haven't eaten in a couple of hours and I'm starving." He pushed her aside.

"Jesus said it is hard for a rich man to enter the Kingdom of Heaven."

He stopped and turned toward her. "The only reason I would want to go to Heaven is I heard the streets are made of gold." He walked away from her and entered the restaurant.

That night, after watching the stock market reports, he went to sleep. He dreamed he was swimming in a pool of liquid gold. Outside the pool, there were several poor people staring at him in awe. He climbed out of the pool, and they all bowed down in front of him. He stepped on each one of their backs as he walked forward. He smiled as everybody worshipped him. With the amount of money he possessed, he was a god. He knew how the Egyptian kings must have felt back in the days of old.

The sound of his alarm woke him from his dream. He slowly climbed out of bed and felt a sharp pain shoot up his foot. He lifted his leg, and a large rock was stuck to the bottom of his right foot. He looked at it closely. It was no ordinary rock. It was a lump of coal.

"What the hell? Is this some sort of joke? Whoever left this here is fired!"

He took a step forward and stepped on another lump of coal. He slowly walked toward the light switch, stepping on another one and then another one. He turned the light on and his whole bedroom floor was covered in lumps of coal. He slowly opened the door, and a large pile of coal fell toward him knocking him backward. He slowly crawled over the pile of coal. He saw no coal on the floor leading to his bathroom. He quickly walked into the bathroom and looked at his reflection in the mirror. His robe, face, and arms were covered in coal dust.

He turned on the faucet. No water came out. He heard a loud clinking sound coming from it. A few seconds later, small pieces of coal fell out. He stepped backward and tripped on a large lump of coal. He fell into the bathtub and felt sharp pains in his back. The whole bathtub was filled completely with large lumps of coal. He struggled to pull himself up. All the walls in his bathroom were covered in coal dust.

He cautiously headed for the kitchen. None of his kitchen staff was in the dining room or in the kitchen. He couldn't find any of his servants anywhere. He grabbed his coat and walked outside. The snow was black. He felt something hit his shoulder. He looked down and saw a large lump of coal by his feet. A large lump of coal hit him in the head. He looked up and saw coal falling from the sky.

"Is this some sort of punishment? It's not my fault I'm filthy rich!"

He could see a large mob of people wearing ratty clothing rushing toward him. He recognized most of them. They were the people he saw the other morning waiting in line at the food bank. They were all carrying large lumps of coal. As they drew nearer, they threw the coal at him. He tried turning the knob on his front door, but it was locked. He screamed as the angry mob pelted him with coal. Each one of the mob's bodies transformed from a human one to a demonic one. He closed his eyes and when he reopened them, he was lying in a fiery pit surrounded by the demons.

"Help me," he pleaded.

The demons laughed and continued to pelt him with lumps of coal for all eternity.

Rosita placed the pillow she had just suffocated Mitt with neatly next to his head. She smiled as she stared at his carcass.

Jared walked over to her and put his arms around her waist. "I know the combination to his safe. We can now afford the dream vacation we've always talk about."

"Merry Christmas," she said and kissed him.

Elvis Has Left the Dead

Author Mark Cusco Ailes opened the totes containing all of his and Derek Ailes' novels while Derek began to set the table up for their latest book signing. Several other authors had showed up for the 2015 Hammond Public Library Local Author's Book Fair. He recognized a majority of them. No matter what book fair they set up at in Northwest Indiana, it was always the same authors. They had become their touring family. All genres were present: children's fiction, romance, paranormal, poetry, and all of the fantasy and horror madness that he and his brother — the Ailes Brothers of Terror — had brought.

With the table setup finally completed, Derek began to take pictures for their official author's website and their Facebook page.

"Take off your Avengers hat. What are you a horror author or a geek?" Mark asked.

"A horror author," Derek answered as he angrily threw his hat into one of the totes exposing his bald head.

The lights in the room flickered briefly as the thunderstorm outside gained momentum.

"How come every time we come to Hammond it storms?" Mark asked.

"Wherever the Ailes Brothers of Terror go, the bad storms follow. Now if only we can get our so-called Facebook friends to follow us as well," Derek said.

The sound of the rain pouring down echoed throughout the room. They both looked concerned since not many people would risk traveling during a severe thunderstorm, especially to a library.

"I guess we should go mingle," Derek suggested.

"Derek, the photographer should be here soon. We shouldn't venture away too long."

Two days earlier, they were interviewed by the local newspaper about their writing career. The photographer was coming to the book fair to get some shots of them selling their books. The newspaper normally didn't do articles about local authors since there were so many. Being they were a horror writing team, they had a brand which most other authors didn't possess. They were popular in Northwest Indiana, and their books were beginning to sell well on Amazon, especially in the UK.

Derek watched as Sandra walked in with her husband who was carrying a cardboard standup of Elvis Presley. She used to hang out with Elvis and wrote a book about him. She had tons of pictures of her and Elvis together.

Derek was only two years old when Elvis died. He always wondered what music he would have recorded if he was still alive in the eighties.

Sandra's husband stood the Elvis standup up and faced it toward the door where it would be the first thing people saw when they entered the room.

The lights in the room went dark for a minute and then came back on. The thunder outside sounded real close.

"Hammond strikes again," Mark said and the other authors laughed. He looked over at Derek, "We better get back to our table."

A couple of families entered the room to hang out with one of the authors. A few people came in after them, but it was relatively dead. One hour into the fair, the reporter came in and immediately took a picture of the Elvis standup. He walked around the room until he found their table and began taking photos. He chatted with Mark and Derek for a few minutes and then left. By the second hour, the storm had passed and people were coming in at a steady pace purchasing books from several authors.

As the book fair came to a close, the authors took down their displays and packed away all of their books. Derek and Mark, satisfied they had another successful book fair selling several books each, walked out of the library to put everything back into their purple PT Cruiser.

"Excuse me, sir," somebody, talking in a way only an Elvis impersonator or Elvis himself would speak, said. "I was wondering if I can chat with you for a second."

The man was dressed in a fancy red costume similar to one of Elvis' flashy outfits and was wearing sunglasses and looked like the Elvis from the sixties. He smelled like Brut.

"Sandra left the building already," Derek said.

"I actually came to see you, Derek of the Ailes Brothers of Terror." He shook his hand, like he was in the middle of a performance, as he spoke.

"You came to see me? I'm more famous than I thought. You sound just like Elvis. You must be a professional impersonator."

"I'm not an impersonator. I'm the real deal," he said and sang "Suspicious Minds" and stopped after a few verses. "I'm here to warn you."

"A warning from Elvis? Is this Candid Camera?" Derek looked around for some cameraman videotaping them from a distance. He looked over at Mark who shrugged his shoulders.

"Let's try to be serious for a moment," Elvis said impatiently. "Derek, you are on a path that will lead you to much peril. In a few days you are going to embark on a path that will have serious repercussions in the future."

"Mark, let me introduce you to the Time-Traveling Elvis," Derek said sarcastically.

"You will eventually be a number one best-selling horror author surpassing Stephen King."

"And this is a bad thing?" Derek said, instantly imagining himself surrounded by millions of fans demanding his autograph. Gorgeous women throwing themselves at his feet. Blockbuster movies being made out all of his novels.

"You will go on an Elvis bashing campaign that will destroy my legacy."

"Sounds like a perfect tradeoff for me. My fame for your fame. Besides, I'm alive and you're dead." Derek looked over at Mark. "Can you imagine hundreds of Derek impersonators?"

Mark cringed at the thought.

Elvis took off his sunglasses and stared Derek straight in the eyes. "I can't allow that to happen."

"Wait a minute!" Mark said. "If you can travel through time, why can't you go into the past and stop yourself from getting hooked on painkillers and prevent your own death?"

"It doesn't work that way. I can't change the past. Only the future. If I could, Elvis Presley would still be here today making hit song after hit song. Now, Derek, I'm giving you just one chance. Do not smear my name." He began to sing "Heartbreak Hotel" and then vanished.

Derek and Mark stood there stunned.

"Did we just encounter Elvis from the grave?" Mark asked.

"And he was no zombie. Why would I go on an Elvis smearing campaign?" Derek asked puzzled. "Let's head on back to Valparaiso. The sky is really dark. I don't think we've seen the last of the severe weather."

The next morning, as Derek uploaded all the photos he took from the book fair onto his official website, he heard a door close. He looked out his window and saw the newspaper carrier place the Sunday edition into the newspaper box by his front door. He ran for the front door in anticipation of reading the article about them. A light blue humming bird was hovering in front of the door and flew away as Derek opened the front door to retrieve the paper. He grabbed the paper and opened it to the second page where the reporter said the article about them would be. The article was there, but to his horror, instead of a picture of the Ailes Brothers of Terror, there was a photo of the cardboard standup of Elvis who had nothing to do with their article.

"Idiot!" Derek screamed.

He ran toward the back bedroom where Mark was at his computer working on his latest novel.

"What's the problem?"

"This!" Derek dropped the paper in front him. "Elvis has stolen our thunder!"

"Where are the photos the photographer took of us?"

"Apparently, nothing says the Ailes Brothers of Terror better than Elvis Presley himself!" Derek started to storm out of Mark's room and stopped. "Elvis will pay for this. I don't care what his warning was. Even if it's the last thing I ever do, I am going to destroy his legacy!" He thought for a few seconds about the best way to accomplish the task. "I'll write the scariest horror novel ever with

Elvis as the psychotic killer. Elvis Presley will be the next Freddy Krueger. The next Jason Voorhees. When they make the movie out of it, Kane Hodder will play Elvis!"

As Derek finished talking, the ground in Graceland shook violently. The large gravestone of Elvis cracked in half and fell into the ground below. A skeleton slowly crawled out of the grave. As the skeleton crawled forward, internal organs began to form, followed by muscles, and then skin and hair until Elvis was once again alive. He snapped his fingers and was wearing his favorite blue outfit. He looked over at his mansion and smiled.

"To the one that brought me back from the dead; thank you, thank you very much." He danced around excitedly. "I think it's time for Elvis to visit Derek in Valparaiso, Indiana, but first, I have a taste for a peanut butter and banana sandwich. Hell, it's been decades since the King has had anything to eat."

Derek, still angry about the newspaper article, wrote a two page blog about how Elvis was overrated and was as good an actor as George W. Bush was as president. He titled the blog post: Hunk of Burning Crap – Derek Ailes Vs Elvis. He posted a picture of Elvis as a zombie which he found searching on Google pictures. Once he finished posting the blog, he began to write his new horror novel: Memphis Damnation.

The next morning, Derek opened the front door to get the newspaper, and the humming bird was back hovering in front of the door. His jaw dropped as he took a closer look at it. The humming bird was wearing a black hair piece and a shiny yellow Elvis costume. It began to sing "Jailhouse Rock". Derek closed the front door and looked out the window. Across the street, his neighbor was mowing his lawn wearing an Elvis costume. He shook his hips as he pushed the lawn mower. Another one of his neighbors was sitting on the front porch dressed as Elvis drinking a Pepsi. His wife was also dressed as Elvis and they were playing Yahtzee.

Derek pinched himself hoping he was dreaming. He looked over at his clock and it was frozen at 8:16 a.m. He heard a car honk its horn repeatedly. He looked outside and saw a 1955 Pink Cadillac Fleetwood parked in front of his house. The door opened and Elvis climbed out pointing at his house. An older man slowly walking down the street with help from his cane approached the car. Elvis put his hand on his shoulder and the old man transformed into an Elvis impersonator.

"Thank you, thank you very much," the impersonator said.

"Don't mention it."

"Love the Cadillac."

"Thanks," Elvis said as the impersonator walked away.

Elvis began to dance his way up to Derek's front door. "Derek, time for us to have a confab. Come outside and face me like a man."

Derek locked the deadbolt.

"I don't need to see you to know you have a yellow stripe down your back!" After a few minutes of waiting impatiently, Elvis went back to his car and grabbed an acoustic guitar and a lawn chair out of the trunk. He placed the lawn chair on the sidewalk and sat down. "I have an eternity to waste and a lot of songs in my repertoire." He sang "That's All Right" and then "Don't Be Cruel" followed by "Return To Sender". After singing several more songs, during which a crowd had gathered around him, he looked at the front door. "Hey, I think it's time to debut my new song "Derek Is A Douchebag."

He stood up and touched each person on the shoulder turning them into an Elvis impersonator. He sat back down and sang:

> There was a coward from Indiana
> Who thought he was the king of the world
> His writings were one dimensional
> No soul would download
>
> A spineless troll he was
> As Charlie Sheen would agree
> There was no hope for Derek
> No fame would he achieve
>
> Such a douchebag
> Such a douchebag

The door opened violently and Derek rushed out of the house. "Enough! I can't take it anymore."

Elvis looked over at his impersonators and with a smile he ordered them to attack. The mob of impersonators rushed at Derek like a horde of hungry zombies. He ran, trying to outrun them, down the street toward Highway 6. As he was close to the Salvation Army Church on the corner, he tripped crashing to the ground. The mob surrounded him and lifted him up over their shoulders. Like someone crowd surfing at a concert, he was passed from one impersonator to another until he was slammed hard onto the ground in front of Elvis.

Elvis smiled sinisterly as he kneeled down in front of him. "Derek, this is your last chance. Stop your anti-Elvis antics."

Derek looked at him with hatred in his eyes. "Never!"

"You leave me no choice," Elvis said and put his right hand on Derek's right shoulder.

Dr. George Nichopoulos led Mark down the long corridor of the Valparaiso Porter-Starke Mental Hospital.

"Is he all right?" Mark asked.

"He's making progress. With further treatment, I think we can help him."

The doctor opened the door to Derek's room. He was sitting in the corner wearing a straitjacket.

"Your brother is here to see you."

Derek, talking in a way only an Elvis impersonator or Elvis himself would speak, said. "Hello, the name's Elvis."

Twisted Twins

Alina stared at all the antique jewelry that was hanging on the rack in the dusty cluttered booth at the flea market. She was looking for something that would go perfectly with her black leather dress and fishnet stockings she wore every Friday at the local nightclub. There were several earrings, but she already owned so many. She was looking for something cool to go along with her gothic wardrobe. There were several necklaces, but none of them seemed to speak to her.

"Can I help you?" an elderly man who looked like Jerry Garcia asked.

"Just browsing through your jewelry. I haven't seen anything beckoning me yet."

"I do have some other necklaces in a box over there. So many antiques and not enough room to display them." He grabbed a large box and placed three necklaces on the table in front of her. One of them was black with a gargoyle shaped medallion with ruby red eyes.

"How much is this one? It's exactly what I'm looking for."

"I can let that one go for ten dollars."

"I'll take it," Alina said excitedly.

She pulled out a ten from her purse and handed it to him. He smiled sinisterly as he took the money from her sending a shiver down her spine.

"Take good care of this one. It will take good care of you."

"Ok."

Alina walked away from the booth as fast as she could. She glanced back to make sure he wasn't following her. After stopping by the food truck outside the flea market to get an elephant ear, she drove home.

She walked into her apartment. Her answering machine was blinking. She pressed the button and listened to her messages.

"Hey, Alina. It's Lucas. Just wanted to know if you wanted to hookup this weekend. Give me a call."

"Just because I slept with you once, doesn't mean I want to do it again. You weren't that great. Been there done that."

She walked into her bedroom and placed the necklace beside the other five she owned. She looked in the mirror and admired herself. She had raven black hair that came down to her shoulders and pale white skin. Her black lipstick and eye shadow matched the black outfit she was wearing. She grabbed the whip she had hanging on the wall and held it in both of her hands.

"On your knees, slave!"

She placed the whip back on its hook and walked into the living room and turned on the television. "American Mary", one of her favorite movies, was on. Katharine Isabelle was so sexy in the movie even she was drooling. After it was over, she took a shower and headed for The Devil's Due where she was a waitress.

"Alina, looking sexy as ever," Skulls, the bouncer, said as she entered the bar.

"Love the new tats."

"Women dig the serpents."

"Maybe you'll score with some hot chick tonight."

"Happily married." Skulls pointed at the wedding ring he wore as a charm on his necklace. He couldn't wear it on his finger because he had a habit of punching rowdy customers in the face when he threw them out of the bar.

"Alina, Lucas is here," Rozalina said in a thick Russian accent and stuck her finger in her mouth in disgust. "How you could have slept with such a troll."

"Lack of self-respect."

"More like bad vodka."

"I don't drink that much."

"You slept with him. You drink too much."

"Ok, I drink too much. Can't party without alcohol."

"Girls, I pay you to serve tables, not jibber-jabber," Mikhail, the bartender, said.

"Mikhail, you are a pridurok," Rozalina said angrily.

"Call me that again and I'll beat your ass!" Mikhail threatened.

"With those tiny hands of yours? I'm so scared."

"Hire Russian women. What was I thinking? Could've hired American women. They have more respect."

"Mikhail, they won't do the things you have us do. If you get my drift."

"Touché."

"I guess I can't avoid Lucas," Alina said.

"If he gives you any trouble, Skulls can beat some respect into him," Mikhail suggested.

"I can handle him — as little as there is of him to handle."

"Ouch," Mikhail said, laughing at the insult.

Alina tied her hair into a bun and sluggishly walked over to Lucas. She wanted to be as unattractive as she possibly could.

"Alina, it's been a while," Lucas said.

He wore a black leather jacket with the Sons of Anarchy emblem on the back. He was a biker wannabe. He was no tough guy. He was as harmless as a little kitten.

"Yes, it has. Why do you frequent a place like this? Applebee's is more your style."

"I come for the wonderful service."

"From Russians? We are all rude here. You, American boy, are just fooling yourself."

"I've missed you."

"Lucas, stop." She stopped using her accent to signify she was being serious. "You are a nice guy. I'm not the get to know me type of girl. I sleep around and that's how I like it. I never sleep with the same guy twice. You understand?"

"Unfortunately, I do."

"Good," she said with her Russian accent. "I'll get you some vodka to make you feel better."

After her shift had finally ended, she purchased a bottle of Vodka from the bar and headed home. She walked into her apartment and quickly shed all of her clothes. She stood in front of her bedroom mirror, completely nude, admiring her body.

"I see why men like me so much." She took a swig from her vodka and stared at her new necklace. "Might as well try you on."

She put it on and admired how it looked against her pale skin. The gargoyle's ruby red eyes glowed brightly. She felt like she was spinning in place and then she passed out.

"Wakey wakey sleepy head," she heard a female voice that sounded like her's say.

She slowly opened her eyes and looked straight at herself. She wasn't looking into her mirror, but she was looking at a spitting image of herself.

"Who are you?" she asked, still feeling very groggy.

"It's me; it's you — however you want to describe yourself or myself."

"Huh?"

"I'm your twin."

"I don't have a twin?"

"You do now."

"I don't understand."

Alina tried to shake off the headache she was feeling.

"Take a sip of your vodka."

Her twin handed her the bottle.

"Is this some sort of Invasion of the Body Snatchers?"

Alina lifted the necklace toward her face and stared at it.

"I'm not here to kill you or take your place. You're the one who put on the necklace."

"I just bought this at the flea market."

"I guess Mr. Grateful Dead should had warned you about its magical powers."

"He said…"

"Take good care of this one. It will take good care of you," they said in unison.

"He didn't say anything about it cloning me, Alina."

"No, you're Alina. I think I'll call myself Athena."

"Athena?"

"Yes, as you can tell, I'm a goddess. Guys will fall at my feet like they do for you. Put some clothes on. Let's go out and have some fun."

"Fun?"

"More like let's go out and get into some trouble — twin style."

Alina stared at her in disbelief. She wasn't sure how to react. *Was this girl really a clone of her or was she something more evil pretending to be her twin?* She'd seen many horror movies in her lifetime and she became skeptical about what was going on here.

Athena, sensing her skepticism, grabbed her arm. "To your laptop. We'll look up the necklace online." She dragged her into the small dining room where her laptop was sitting on a small table. She did a search for the gargoyle necklace. On the Cursed Relics website, there was a small article about it. "The necklace has the ability to create a complete clone of those who wears it."

Alina read the article over Athena's shoulder.

"Says nothing bad about the clone." Athena smiled at her. "Now let's go have some fun."

"What do you have in mind?"

"Party! Get wasted! Pick up some men! The usual stuff!" She danced around the kitchen.

"Not too much fun. We have to… I mean I have to work tonight."

"Do you think Mikhail would hire me?"

"Maybe we shouldn't tell anybody I know about you."

"Why? None of them really know anything about our family in Russia. They don't really know if you have a twin sister or not. You've never told them anything about your personal life outside the different guys we've, I mean you've, slept with."

"Ok, I'll introduce you. He'll probably get a kick out of having two of us working there. Twin Russian gothic chicks will probably bring in some more clientele."

"Some guys have twin fantasies."

"Athena, maybe we should set some boundaries."

"No, Alina. We aren't at that part of our relationship yet."

"Athena!"

"I'm kidding. I know you have a better sense of humor than that since we share the same sense of humor."

"We better get going."

"Maybe you should put some clothes on first."

Athena pointed toward her naked body.

"That would have been awkward," Alina said and walked into her bedroom.

They walked into Death Metal Hell, the nightclub down the street from The Devil's Due. The music was loud and the place was filled almost to capacity with metal heads. The place smelled like marijuana. Within seconds, they were hit on by several guys as they squeezed through the crowd toward the bar.

"Two vodkas," Alina said to the bald, muscular bartender with tattoos all over his neck and forehead.

"Look at all the man meat out there. I guess we won't be needing any toys tonight," Athena joked.

"You're bad."

"Alina, you're thinking it, too."

"You're perverted."

"So are you."

"Can I buy both of you girls a drink?" A tall, muscular, blond man with skull tattoos all over his arms asked.

"You can pay for our vodkas," Athena answered. "This one's mine, Alina."

"You two interested in a private party?"

"What type of private party?" Alina asked.

"Booze, drugs. Only the best stuff." As he was talking, his friend dropped a roofie in both of their vodkas.

"Sounds like our type of party," Athena said.

Alina took a large gulp of her vodka and began to dance around in a circle while Athena cheered her on. As she was dancing, she began feeling lightheaded and passed out.

Alina opened her eyes and was back in her apartment. Athena was sitting on the chair next to the couch smiling at her. As her eyes adjusted to the light, she could see that Athena's hands and clothes were covered in blood.

"What happened?"

"Alina, the guys thought they could knock us out and take advantage of us." The smile on her face grew bigger. "What they didn't realize was the drug had no effect on me."

"Whose blood is that?"

"Why theirs."

"What did you do?" Alina asked angrily.

"Come, I'll show you."

She followed her into the bathroom. She stared at the horrific sight in shock.

"Beautiful isn't it. I was going to go for the human centipede, but decided Siamese twins were more appropriate."

From a scene right out of "American Mary", the two guys were sown together with black thread. Lying on the floor besides them were two of their legs and arms. She brought over a giant glass jar filled with liquid and their appendages.

"Their family jewels," Athena laughed sinisterly.

"You're sick."

Alina stepped backward out of the bathroom.

"Where are you going?"

"Away from you! You're insane!"

"Alina, you're just as sick and demented as I am. You would have done the same thing."

"No, Athena. I could never harm someone like that."

As Athena moved toward her, she continued to step backward.

"Why are you so afraid of me? We are one in the same. Identical down to the last cell."

Alina ripped the necklace away from her neck as she continued to step backward, not realizing the window was opened behind her. She tripped backward. Athena ran forward to grab her before she fell out the window. She grabbed her right hand which slowly began to slip away since her hands were still covered in the blood of the two guys she operated on. As she lost her grip, Alina fell to her death; her head splattering on the pavement below.

"Oh crap," Athena said as she watched her own body slowly disappear.

Rozalina was heading home from the Devil's Due to get stoned after scoring some cocaine from a client earlier. She was nearing Alina's apartment when she saw her fall to her death. She quickly ran over to her as the blood flowed around her skull.

"Alina, suicide? Why? You had such as great life," she cried as she kneeled over her body.

She saw the necklace with the eyes from the gargoyle medallion glowing bright red beckoning her. She put her hands around it feeling its warmth. She felt like it was meant for her and it was telling her it would fill the void in her meaningless life.

"Alina, I don't think you'll be needing this anymore," she said as she grabbed it and walked away.

Marriage Zquality

Franklin watched Matilda as she slept on her queen-sized bed with satin sheets. Her greyish-blonde hair flowed down over her slightly pale grey skin. During the zombie apocalypse of 2015, she was bitten by their daughter, Nancy, who had turned into a zombie after being bitten by one of her teachers at the South Haven Elementary School. He had been forced to shoot his daughter in the head with his hunting rifle. After several days of fighting the infection, Matilda had passed away. While at the coroner's office, she was injected with an experimental drug which, when she came back to life as a zombie, killed the zombie infection almost instantly. His girlfriend returned to being the loving, caring woman she had always been, and not some flesh hungry mindless zombie.

He felt so lucky to still have her in his life. They had been living together, unmarried, for several years before the zombie apocalypse. They always wanted to get married, but kept putting it off while both tried to establish themselves in their respective fields while also trying to raise a family. They now wanted to get married, but the States would not allow a human and a zombie to legally marry. Since zombies were now a large percentage of the population, the Undeadagains as they were named by the politicians and religious groups, there was a movement to legalize marriage between humans and zombies.

He walked out of the bedroom and sat in front of the television. Reverend Ronald Dukakis was on Fox News talking about the Undeadagains and their desire to have their right to marry case brought before the Supreme Court.

"Marriage is the union between a man and a woman. If these Undeadagains gain their right to marry, then it is blasphemy. I will set myself on fire."

"Are you serious?" News Anchor Steve Russo asked.

"You heard me. Mark my words. I will set myself on fire."

"And I have plenty of lighter fluid," Franklin laughed and turned the channel to watch a repeat of iZombie.

"Franklin, I'm hungry," Matilda said as she sat down next to him wearing her pink pajamas covered with pictures of cats playing with balls of yarn.

"Brains?"

"Stop being silly," she said and slapped his right shoulder. "I want bacon and scrambled eggs."

"Coming right up."

"Ooh, iZombie. I love this show."

Russo Jones, a scientist and Republican at heart, stared in disbelief at the newscast on CNN about the possibility the Supreme Court would rule in the zombies' favor. Four states had passed a law making the union between humans and zombies legal; ironically, the same states that made pot legal.

"This is not right in the eyes of God. First same sex marriages were legalized, now zombies. What's next? Will men be allowed to legally marry their pets? This has to be stopped."

Russo walked across his lab toward a large steel cage imprisoning a short brunette with long black hair with silver streaks. She was beautiful despite her greyish-brown skin. She possessed a body that even he couldn't help drooling over.

"Please, let me go. I'm a human being," she pleaded.

"No, you are not. You are a demon possessing this poor creature's body. Only a parasite inhabiting a soulless body."

"Have some compassion."

"Compassion for what? You are no different than a lab rat and thus should be treated as such. Besides, you will serve a purpose for my cause."

She stared at him angrily.

"Even though you didn't ask, I'll tell you what your purpose will be anyway. I have taken the zombie strain and mutated it. Once I inject it into you, you will become a flesh craving zombie and not the peaceful one you are now. With your help, the zombie apocalypse will return and the general population will have no choice but to round every one of you up and kill you. There will be no Supreme Court ruling in your favor. It will be as it should remain, a union between a man and a woman."

"Your plan will fail."

"No, my dear, it won't."

Olivia placed the bags of groceries in the truck for the customer of Mega-Mart. With the task finished, she walked back toward the entrance of the grocery store. She was an eighteen year old blonde teenager. Her grey-skin shined in the sunlight. Her boyfriend, Willis, had rushed her to the hospital after she had been bitten by a zombie at Mega-Mart, and she was injected with the vaccine. She loved him with all of her heart and hoped someday she could marry him. She was so happy that people welcomed her with open arms after her ordeal. If she hadn't been vaccinated, she surely would had eaten her boyfriend.

She always joked with him saying he was yummy, that only a dimwitted zombie would pass his flesh up. He didn't find it as funny as she did, but she teased him about it on a daily basis anyway.

She could see dark clouds in the distance. A severe storm was brewing that would give Valparaiso a minor reprieve from the roaring heat wave they had been experiencing for the past couple weeks.

"Clean up in Aisle 3."

"A zombie's job is never done," she sighed as she walked to the backroom to grab a mop.

After a hearty breakfast, Franklin and Matilda went out for a jog before the severe weather reached Portage. After trying to keep up with his marathon runner of a girlfriend, he stopped to rest in front of the South Haven Public Library.

"Getting too old to keep up? Hell, I'm half past dead and can run circles around you," Matilda joked.

"You were always in better shape." He tried catching his breath. "I just need a few minutes rest."

"We can't rest too long unless you want to get drenched."

"The rain sounds good about now. I'm sweating up a storm."

"That is an advantage of being zombiefied. I never sweat," she said with a smile.

"A comedian to the better end and beyond."

"Now that's funny."

"I thought you'd like it. Race you back home."

"I think maybe a fast stroll back. I don't think your heart will be able to handle it."

"Thanks for the vote of confidence."

"More like caution. Our house is a mile back that way past the highway."

"I'll be fine."

"I'll let you lead and set the pace."

He began to jog increasing his speed.

"I knew that would motivate you."

"When we get home, I'll show you how motivated I am."

"Dirty pervert. I like it."

She jogged past him and waved.

Russo carried a syringe filled with glowing green serum over to the cage. The girl slammed her head into the back of the cage as she tried to move away from him. He reached in, grabbed her left arm, and pulled her toward him. She screamed and tried to bite him.

"Not yet. You need to be re-infected before that will be affective."

"Screw you!"

He twisted her arm violently and injected it with the serum. She began to cry as she realized her fate.

"In a matter of minutes, the virus will re-take its hold on you. When you awake, you will go on a flesh eating rampage. You are going to be referred to as Patient Re-Zero."

"You're going to be my first victim."

"Trust me; you will be no threat to me. I'll be locked in here safe. I have plenty of provisions to see it through until the government gets the zombie apocalypse back under control."

"You're insane."

"Thanks for the compliment," she heard him say as she passed out.

When she awoke, she was standing in the middle of a park hungry for human flesh.

Franklin and Matilda hid in their underground shelter he had installed in his backyard several months back after the zombie apocalypse had ended. It cost all of his savings and the money in his IRA to build, but he wanted to be prepared if there ever was another zombie outbreak. They watched the news on the television.

"Thanks to the rapid response from the United States Government and its military, the recent outbreak from the zombie virus has been contained. The President has assured us that there remains no further threats and people can resume their every day to day lives. With us is Reverend Ronald Dukakis. Reverend are we in fact safe?"

"By no means are we safe from any further zombie outbreaks. As long as there are still Undeadagains in our midst, the threat of an outbreak remains. I urge all citizens who are harboring these heathens to bring them to the nearest government facilities and have them disposed of. They are a threat to society and our well-being."

"That's bullshit!" Matilda screamed.

"I would never do that," Franklin assured her.

"It's not you I'm worried about. It's our neighbors, our family, and our friends. This is Nazi Germany all over again."

"They aren't going round up all the Undeadagains and take them to some sort of concentration camp."

"That's what it sounds like he's recommending. Listen to him."

"Reverend, how do you think this incident is going to influence the Supreme Court's decision on the Human/Zombie marriage act?"

"After the recent outbreak, I believe that is off the table. Undeadagains are the work of the devil and should be sent back to Hell where they belong. They don't deserve any rights. They aren't human."

"Turn it off," Matilda said, crying.

"Matilda, I won't let them take you. We'll live down here for the rest of our lives if we have to."

"What type of life will that be?"

"As long as we're together, it will be a great one."

"What if they come for me?"

"Then I'll kill anyone who tries to take you."

Olivia stood in front of her bathroom mirror crying. She stared at her greyish face. She had just watched the interview with the Reverend and was scared. Last week, she had witnessed her neighbors on a zombie hunting streak bringing back the zombies' heads as trophies. Willis had been with her through the ordeal making sure she wouldn't be a target during the recent zombie purge.

"Olivia!"

"Willis, I'm in the bathroom."

Willis walked up the stairs and stopped in front of the door staring at her. He walked in and held her in his arms.

"The Reverend is a douchebag," he stated.

"What if people believe him? All of us could be in danger. You saw the vicious way our neighbors tortured and murdered all of those zombies."

"They were mindless zombies. You are not."

"I don't think it will make much of a difference now. There is hatred toward my kind."

"What are you talking about — your kind. You are human like the rest of us."

"No, I'm not. Look at me. My skin is grey and my hair is white."

"You are as beautiful as the day I first met you."

"You're an idiot."

She began to cry, but stopped when she heard loud pounding on the front door.

"Where is she?" Travis, their next door neighbor, shouted.

The pounding got fierce.

"Lock the door. Do not unlock it no matter what."

"Willis, don't go."

Travis stopped pounding as his buddy, Jay ran over to him with his shotgun.

"Are you ready?" Travis asked.

"Yep."

Travis violently kicked the door open and Jay ran in ready to kill. Willis slowly walked down the stairs.

"Willis, we like you. Stand aside!" Travis ordered.

"No, this is not your house."

"The devil is in this house and the devil must die," Travis said angrily.

Jay pointed the gun toward Willis.

"I won't let you harm her."

Jay fired the weapon at Willis causing him to fall down the rest of the stairs and bleed out onto the living room floor. They heard the bathroom door close.

"She's upstairs. Jay, you know what to do."

"It's killing time!"

Travis followed Jay up the stairs. He kicked the bathroom door open and Jay shot Olivia in the chest knocking her to the ground. She looked up at them with tears in her eyes. "May God forgive you both."

"May the devil embrace you with open arms," Jay said and shot her in the head.

Franklin sat next to Matilda as she ate the turkey sandwich he had made for her. She hadn't watched television in days since the news was filled with horrific stories about the Undeadagain purge that was taking place across the nation. People had gone completely insane killing them and those harboring them. To protect herself from going completely insane, she began to write in a diary about her life since becoming an Undeadagain and going into hiding. So far, they had been left alone because nobody really knew about their underground shelter since their nearest neighbor was down the road. Eventually, the government would show up looking for her since she was listed as an Undeadagain on her driver's license.

"Maybe you should walk outside and breathe some fresh air. It's getting dark outside. We should be safe."

"Franklin, we can't risk it."

"Ok, but tomorrow I'm going to have to do some grocery shopping."

"Just bring back plenty of chips. I get bored down here. I've watched every DVD we own and my eyes can't handle reading another book in this synthetic light."

"I can bring the PlayStation down here, and you can play some video games."

"Bring all the games down."

"I will."

He sat down next to her and put his arm around her. He kissed her forehead. He thought about the times they had together before the apocalypse. She was very strong willed, one of the reasons he fell in love with her. There was nothing that could stand in her way. No matter what the obstacle had been, she overcame it.

"I love you."

"Franklin, I know," she said with a smile. "Do you want to make love to me?"

"It would pass the time."

"There isn't anything else to do down here," she said and kissed him.

The next morning, Franklin left to do the grocery shopping. While he was away, Matilda continued to write in her diary. She heard a loud sound outside. *Franklin just left. It couldn't be him.* She climbed out of bed and walked over to the wooden stairs leading to the door above. She could hear several voices outside. She stood still staring forward as the door burst inward and three police officers dressed in riot gear rushed in with their guns pointed straight at her.

She just stared at them as they opened fire.

Franklin pulled into his driveway a couple hours later. He grabbed the bags of groceries and walked toward his backyard. He dropped the groceries as he spotted the door leading into the shelter smashed inward. He ran through the doorway and saw the floor covered in blood. Matilda was nowhere to be seen. Sitting on top of the bed was her diary. He grabbed it, skimming through it until he came to the last page with writing.

On the bottom of the page, written in someone else's handwriting, it read: Purge Completed.

In the Hollies Style

Allan stood in front of the old restaurant waiting for the bus to arrive. It had been pouring down rain for several minutes and he wished he had grabbed his umbrella before leaving his apartment a couple hours earlier. The bus was running fifteen minutes late and he was in a hurry to get to his friend, Graham's, house to record a couple of songs he wrote the night before. He, Graham, Bernie, Bobbie, and Tony had been working on a bunch of demos hoping a record company would be interested in signing them.

A tall woman with long, curly blonde hair wearing a black dress walked over to him. She was protected from the pouring rain by a red umbrella. He quickly glanced at her trying not to be obvious that he was checking her long tanned legs out. She stood next to him also waiting for the bus.

"Hi," she said seductively.

"Hi," he said, trying not to sound shy.

She smiled. There was something about his scent she liked. It reminded her of a man she knew a long time ago. She knew he was the man she was looking for.

"You can stand under my umbrella. But seeing how drenched you are, I don't think it will make much of a difference now," she laughed.

"Don't mind if I do." He moved closer to her, under the protection of the umbrella.

"My name's Allan."

"Carrie-Anne."

"Nice to make your acquaintance."

She looked at him, checking him out. Her stomach growled loudly. Embarrassed she said, "I haven't eaten in a long time. Work has been keeping me busy."

"What do you do?"

"I work at the museum preparing antiques for display."

She tried really hard to stop her stomach from growling. She was hungry and Allan looked delicious.

"This may sound like a strange question. What is your blood type?"

"Huh? I'm not sure."

"It really doesn't matter."

A blood-red smile crossed her lips, revealing two ivory fangs and an endless hunger.

Allan jumped back out of fear and began to walk backward.

"What are you?"

"Some would refer to me as a vampire."

She moved slow and sensual, stalking her prey in delight. As she was licking her lips, Allan turned and ran. She was about to chase after him when she spied a homeless guy lying on the ground next to a dumpster.

"I guess you'll have to do. I'm in no mood to run today. Another time, Allan. Another time."

"A vampire? You didn't try any of that funky weed, did ya?" Graham asked, trying not burst into a fit of laughter. "I guess you should start carrying garlic with you."

"Graham, I'm not joking. It really happened."

"I would believe you being a vampire. You look like a tall, thin Dracula," Bernie joked.

"I want to bite your neck," Bobbie said, trying to sound like Dracula.

"You won't be laughing if you encounter her," Allan promised him.

"That's all we need — some blood thirsty groupie," Bernie laughed.

The door burst open and Tony rushed in. "Come listen to this song on the radio!"

They walked into Graham's living room and "Love Me Do" by the Beatles was playing.

"They were saying this group is the future of the industry," Tony explained.

"Allan, do you think we can replicate their sound?" Graham asked.

"I believe we can make it better," Allan promised.

After the song ended, Graham looked at Allan with the most serious look he had ever possessed. "Let's go rehearse the new songs. By the way, Allan, no songs about vampires."

"Fine. It really happened. Let's rehearse."

After rehearsing for several hours, they made their way to their favorite pub to throw darts and drink until they couldn't stand up straight.

"Don't let us run out," Bernie said to the waitress.

"Do I ever?" she said as she walked away.

"I was thinking about how I escaped death today," Allan said as he threw a dart, hitting the bullseye.

"Here we go again." Graham shook his head.

"I'm serious. Her stomach was growling and she was going to eat me."

"Allan has quite an imagination. A perfect trait for a songwriter," Bobbie said while tapping his drumsticks on the table in perfect rhythm with the song playing on the jukebox.

As they were talking, the door to the pub opened and four men wearing black trench coats walked in. Allan dropped his beer mug in horror as Carrie-Anne walked in behind them still wearing the same black dress.

"Guys, it's her." Allan said, shaking nervously.

"Looks like plenty to go around," the tallest of the men said, licking his lips in anticipation.

"Can I get you guys something to drink?" the waitress asked.

The man spun around and grabbed her throat, lifting her up several feet. He quickly bit into her neck causing blood to flow outward. Her blood was hot and salty upon his tongue and he gulped greedily.

The bartender grabbed his shotgun from underneath the bar. Before he could lift it up to shoot, one of the other men was on him biting into his neck.

"Hello, Allan. I followed your scent here. I'm glad your friends are here to join me for dinner....literally." Carrie-Anne walked toward them.

"Guys, do you think we can win in a bar fight?" Bernie asked.

"Against vampires, are you nuts?" Graham replied.

"Back door leads to the alleyway," Bobbie suggested.

Tony grabbed a pool stick and snapped it in half. He walked backward and tripped over a chair. One of the men lunged for him and before he could land on him, Tony jabbed the end of the pool cue into his chest. The man looked at him stunned, and then burst into flames and crumbled into ash.

"Grab a weapon and aim for their chests," Bobbie commanded and held his drumsticks ready to strike.

"What are you going to do, drum me to death?" the tallest man laughed. He stood in front of Bobbie taunting him. "I'll let you take the first shot."

Bernie grabbed a beer mug and slammed it in the back of the tall man's head. As he turned around to attack him, Bobbie stabbed him with one of the drumsticks. The tall man screamed angrily, burst into flames, and crumbled to ash.

Carrie-Anne turned her attention away from Allan and watched as his friends killed all of the other vampires. She looked back at Allan angrily.

"Another time, my sweet."

She rushed out of the pub, transformed into a bat, and flew away.

"Ok, you were telling the truth," Graham said as he tried to catch his breath.

"How can ordinary pieces of wood pierce their skin so easily?" Bobbie asked as he stared at his drumsticks.

"It's because you all are reincarnations of vampire slayers from a long time ago," a short, stocky man wearing a grey business suit said from the back of the bar.

"Who are you?" Graham asked.

"I've been referred to by many names over the centuries, but you can call me Ronnie. Not only am I a music producer, I am also a vampire slayer. I was sent by my record label, Parlophone, to offer you a record deal."

"Record deal right after we were almost killed?" Tony questioned.

"The record company is a front for us vampire slayers. We've been looking for a while for the ones who will wipe the vampire race from existence. You guys are the ones."

"We are vampire slayers?" Bernie looked at him suspiciously.

"You can easily slay any vampire with whatever you hold that is made out of wood. Come with me to the recording studio. I will make you a famous music group and you can kill vampires for us while making yourselves richer than your wildest dreams."

"Ronnie, you've got the wrong guys. We're musicians, not slayers," Allan told him.

"Trust me, she'll be back with reinforcements. She has your scent. She'll be able to find you no matter where you go," he warned. "I will teach you everything you need to know to protect yourself from her vampire order."

"And you'll make us rich in the process?" Tony asked.

"Yes, I promise you."

Allan looked at each of them and then at Ronnie. "We're in."

Bobbie sat down behind his drum set inside the recording studio while Graham and Allan talked with Ronnie outside.

"The powers that be want your first single to be a guaranteed hit. They want you to cover The Coasters' song '(Ain't That) Just Like Me'. Do it in your own style."

"We are familiar with the tune. I've always liked the catchy chorus," Graham said.

"We actually have also played 'Searchin' at some of our gigs," Allan added.

"Excellent. We'll record them both. Two guaranteed hits," Ronnie said excitedly.

"Let's do it." Graham said as he led Allan into the studio.

"Guys were doing '(Ain't That) Just Like Me'. Let's hit it from the top." Bobbie kicked it off as Allan began to sing his heart out.

For the next few years, they recorded and toured extensively while battling vampires on a nightly basis. Going on with as little sleep as they could, they fought and killed hundreds of vampires, but they hadn't seen Carrie-Anne since the night in the pub. Graham even recorded a song titled "Carrie-Anne" hoping to draw her out of hiding. During that time, both Allan and Graham had met women who they married.

Trying to keep up with his marriage, constant touring, and killing vampires, Graham was wearing down quickly. After their latest album "King Midas in Reverse" failed to chart, and his disagreement with the rest of the band about doing a Bob Dylan cover album, Graham decided it was time to retire from the vampire slaying and move to America to join up with the friends he met while touring there, Stephen and David, and form a new folk rock band.

Allan watched as his friend boarded the plane heading for the States. He sat down and watched the plane take off. He thought about all the good and bad times he and Graham had experienced since their childhood. Neither of them ever imagined the impact on the music industry they would grow up to have. Let alone all the vampires they would slay.

A familiar voice from behind snapped him out of his trance. "Hello, Allan. It's been a long time."

Allan quickly spun around holding a wooden stake in his hand ready to strike. "Carrie-Anne."

"Is that how you say hello to a dear old friend?" She sat down and stared up at him. Her fangs ached for his throat, but she ignored her hunger. "Put that thing away before you draw unwanted attention to us."

"What do you want?" He put it back into the holster he wore as a belt.

"To warn you of things to come. Now that your group is falling apart at the seams, I thought it would be the opportune time to reappear from my hibernation. Yes, I've been asleep for years waiting for the perfect time to awake from my slumber. Charging up my batteries, as the saying goes."

"You know I'll have to kill you."

Carrie-Anne laughed for several seconds before looking at him with her cold dead eyes. "Good luck with that. By the way, I think your wife is beautiful." She transformed into a bat and flew away.

Allan sat there stunned. Outside the window, he could see several bats sitting watching him. He grabbed several wooden stakes off of his holster and walked out of the terminal toward them. Salivating, they transformed back into their human forms and stared at him.

"Tonight I'm in a killing mood." Allan said.

He deflected the attack from one of the vampires while stabbing another one in the chest. Several more bats landed, transforming into vampires, surrounding him.

Allan jumped to the side as a large black van with wooden stakes attached to the hood, the roof, and the sides collided into the group of vampires impaling several of them. Bobbie, Tony, and Bernie jumped out of the van after it stopped and attacked the vampires killing what was left of them. Tony ran over to Allan and helped him back to his feet.

"Carrie-Anne is back." Allan looked at them concerned.

"Ronnie warned us. We got here as quick as we could."

"Thanks. As you can see, I was greatly outnumbered. With only four of us now, we will need to be more cautious."

"We will be back to five tomorrow. Ronnie hired a replacement for us. His name is Terry."

"I hope he knows what he's getting himself into." Allan placed his wooden stakes back into the holster. "Singing is one thing. Killing a vampire is another."

"Agreed" they said in unison.

"She knows about my wife."

"Don't worry, Allan. Ronnie has her locked away safe. She's already complaining about the strong garlic smell," Tony assured him.

"That's a relief."

The next several months, they didn't see Carrie-Anne or the vampires anywhere. They took the free time to begin working on a new studio album. They entered the studio and a man wearing gigantic sunglasses was sitting behind a piano working on some music.

"Hey Reg, it's been awhile," Allan said excitedly.

"Actually, I go by the name Elton John now. My manager advised me it was in my best interest to come up with a stage name to further my music career. I came up with it as a tribute to two great musicians: Elton Dean and Long John Baldry."

"It is catchy."

"I think with my piano sound, your song is going to be a major hit."

"He Ain't Heavy has lyrics which moves me in here." Allan pointed toward his heart.

"I felt it too when I rehearsed it."

1970 was one of the best years so far since Graham had left. With three consecutive hits, the band was back in the spotlight. In the States, their latest album was climbing the charts. Allan was at the pub watching Tony and Terry write some new songs. He couldn't remember a time they weren't composing when they weren't vampire slaying.

The vampires were also kept busy in 1970. They were assembling signifying Carrie-Anne was preparing to strike in one massive attack.

Allan wanted to end the fight with Carrie-Anne once and for all. The days of touring and slaying vampires were taking its toll on him. He didn't possess the energy he had years prior. Secretly, he was unhappy and wanted to try a solo career. Terry was doing more of the lead vocals on the albums and Allan believed his time with the band was almost over. He promised to do one more studio album with them and then he would let them know he wanted out.

The door to the pub opened and Bobbie and Bernie rushed in.

"Allan, Carrie-Anne was spotted in the mountains. Our spies have reported thousands of vampires merging on her location," Bobbie informed him.

"Grab every weapon we have. Have Ronnie order the spike tanks to rendezvous with us there. We will finally get a chance to use them in battle," Allan ordered.

"I know the odds are against us and we are facing certain death, but I'm really excited," Terry said.

"We end this tonight. I promise by night's end, Carrie-Anne will be dead." Allan led them out of the pub toward their black van.

All five of their spiked tanks rolled toward the mountains followed by hundreds of archers trained for battling vampires. The tanks were designed to shoot hundreds of wooden stakes at a time. Parlophone had spent a large chunk of its profits modifying the tanks for vampire slaying. Ronnie sat in the main tank communicating with the other four, strategizing the attack.

"I see them up ahead. When we are in range fire," Ronnie ordered.

When the tanks were close enough, they fired hundreds of wooden stakes killing hundreds of the vampires who were caught off guard. As the tanks were reloading, the archers fired the spiked wooden arrows.

Kelief, Carrie-Anne's lead advisor, rushed into her chamber. "We are under attack! They caught us off guard. They have tanks."

"Destroy their tanks. I don't care how many lives we lose. Their army must not reach my lair. Tonight I kill Allan and his bandmates. Then, nobody will be in our way. The vampires will be able to take over the world unopposed."

"Yes, your highness."

"Allan, my sweet Allan. Soon I will get to taste the blood I've been hungering for since we first met." She sat down on her golden throne and watched the battle outside through the magic orb standing next to her.

Tony navigated their black van through the middle of the vampire army. The wiper blades couldn't keep up with all the black ash covering the windshield from the dying vampires, as the van's wooden spikes penetrated the vampires they were driving through.

"I can see an opening in the mountain ahead. When we stop, jump out of the van immediately and kill every vampire in our path. I must get to her," Allan instructed.

"Good luck, everybody," Terry added.

"We're definitely going to need it," Bobbie said as Tony slammed the breaks. They jumped out of the van and began the assault on the vampires.

Carrie-Anne slammed the orb to the ground smashing it into hundreds of tiny pieces. "How can my army be so useless against mortals? Come after me if you can, Allan! You haven't witnessed my true form yet!"

Allan broke through the vampire army as his bandmates slaughtered every one of them in their path. Tony signaled to him to go ahead and they'd hold them off. Allan entered the opening of the mountain and cautiously walked down the long corridor inward. Ahead of him, Kelief stood cracking his knuckles, loosening himself for combat.

"I want Carrie-Anne!"

"For several years, I heard about you and your band of misfits and your heroic deeds. You aren't the human race's saviors; you're the vampire's butchers. You see, we vampires didn't start the war. You humans did. Believe me, we are the ones who will finish it," Kelief said as he swung a large ax in front of him displaying his strength.

"A vampire wielding an ax. Now that's a new one."

"This was our weapon of choice back in the old days before our thirst for blood. It was brought on by a curse put on our kind a long time ago by a witch when vampires and man joined together to rid the world of their kind. I claimed this ax as a prize from a dear old friend I was forced to kill in battle. It's fitting now because man will be completely erased from time by us vampires."

"I thought Graham talked too much. Can I kill you now or do I have to listen to your history lesson?"

"Very well."

Kelief swung the ax toward Allan who ducked barely missing being decapitated. He swung again as Allan rolled to the right.

"Give up now. I can swing the ax for eternity if I have to."

"And miss for eternity."

Kelief rushed him and Allan grabbed his arm. The two men fought over the ax, each grabbing hold of the handle. Kelief forcefully pushed Allan backward and lifted the ax high above his head. As Kelief swung again, Allan jumped over the ax and plunged two large stakes into his chest. Kelief dropped the ax in horror. His body burst into flames and then crumbled into ash.

Allan picked up the ax. It felt familiar to him as if he had held it before. He remembered when they had first met Ronnie and he told them they were reincarnations of vampire slayers from the past. This was his ax from back in the time when man and vampires were allies before the witch put the curse of blood thirst on the vampires. Kelief and he had been friends and it was Kelief who killed him and claimed his ax as a prize. He remembered when the ax was blessed by the water from the sacred well in his village. It possessed the power to kill vampires. He smiled as he realized he possessed the weapon that could defeat Carrie-Anne for good.

He walked forward remembering the layout of the mountain from when he had been there in the past. Her lair was in the middle of the mountain and Kelief had taken his life there.

Carrie-Anne stood before him dressed in the shiny black dress she wore when she first walked into the pub years back. She grabbed her blonde hair and ripped it and her face completely off, exposing a face that looked centuries old. She raised her arms and transformed into a large bat-like creature, which was the size of a large dragon with a large tail. Her skin was dark brown and looked to be as impenetrable as a dragon's.

"This is my true form! My real name is Belykial and it is I, by that name, who will kill!"

Belykial swung her tail around in a fast spinning motion knocking him to the ground. The ax slid out of his hand and landed on the other side of the lair.

"Now you must fight me with your bare hands!"

The ground shook violently with each of her steps sending large rocks tumbling downward. She laughed loudly as she watched him try to avoid them.

"Death by compression! Now that would be a tragic ending for you!"

He jumped up and ran for the other side of the lair. She stomped down violently causing the ground to crack. Her throne fell inward as the ground gave way. His ax slid forward stopping inches from falling over the edge of the newly formed hole. As she stomped again, he slid across the ground grabbing the ax. He grabbed onto the back of her tail avoiding falling into the hole. She lifted her tail up several feet and violently slammed it downward. He held on tightly. As the tail landed again, he quickly climbed it and swung the ax upward slicing one of her claws off. She screamed. He swung the ax repeatedly slicing into her chest. She tried flicking him off with her other claw, but he continued to dodge it.

"Stop it, human!"

She brought her massive head down preparing to rip him in half in one bite. As her head got nearer, he swung the ax upward and it embedded into her skull. She knocked him to the side and screamed out in agony as her body shrunk back into her human form.

"Please don't kill me," she pleaded.

"I must."

He grabbed one of his wooden spikes and implanted it into her heart. She screamed out one last time as her body burst into flames and she crumbled into dust.

As she died, all the remaining vampires in the world instantly burst into flames and crumbled into dust, as well.

Several weeks later, Allan was in the pub with some of the friends he met since the battle with Carrie-Anne, writing a song for the last studio album before leaving the band.

"Come on, it's your turn. I'm going to beat you this time."

"I only have a couple lines left to write."

He wrote down the lyrics:

'Cause that long cool woman had it all
Had it all
Had it all

With the song finished, he smiled. Only a select few would really understand the words behind the song. Each line symbolized the events leading to his first meeting with Carrie-Anne and to her demise. He put down his pen and grabbed his darts. There was no way he was going to let his friend beat him at darts.

The end?

Claws Vs Mecha Cat

Chapter One

Melvin and Denise stood on the platform at the Dunes Park train station surrounded by several people waiting for the South Shore Line to arrive. They were anxiously waiting for the train to take them to the McCormick Place for the 2015 Chicago Auto Show.

There was a chime from the speakers above followed by an automated message stating the westbound train would be arriving in ten minutes.

Melvin smiled at his wife as he anticipated the train ride. He loved taking the train to their yearly visit to the Chicago Auto Show. The ride was not much of a scenic route mostly one rundown ghetto after another. At least, they would pass the Railcats stadium. Unfortunately, it was February and there wouldn't be any games being played.

A couple of older gentlemen were talking about how Smart cars were a joke and real men drove gas-guzzling trucks. He wasn't a fan of them either. He wanted a brand new Colorado truck, but Denise wanted to own a car practical for raising a family. They both possessed decent paying jobs, and he didn't see any reason why they couldn't afford both, but she kept reminding him she wanted to buy a fancy house in Chesterton with five bedrooms, one for each of the four kids she wanted to have.

He jumped in excitement when he saw the train's headlights in the distance.

"Take it down a notch, Melvin. We are grownups," Denise said, smiling.

"For now. No promises when we get to the Auto Show."

"As long as you're there to look at the cars, not the models."

"Denise, do I hear a tiny bit of jealously?"

"Your days of shopping around are over. You made your final purchase." She pointed at her wedding ring.

The train stopped in front of them and they entered the front car. They sat down on the first available seat. He was disappointed as he realized they were sitting opposite of the way the train was heading. They would be seeing things as they passed them.

Noticing his disappointment, Denise said sarcastically, "At least if there's a train wreck, we won't see it coming."

He gave her a disapproving look.

"Ok, that was in bad taste."

"Do ya' think?"

The doors to the train car closed and the train moved forward. "Next stop Ogden Dunes," the conductor said through the intercom system.

"Get the tickets out," Melvin reminded her.

Denise thumbed through her purse until she found the train tickets. Melvin looked at all of the train cars sitting in front of the steel mill as they passed by. The fog was thick today making it difficult to see the individual buildings of the mill. Through the fog, he thought he saw something moving, something big.

"What the hell?"

"Melvin, what's wrong?"

"That." He pointed toward the fog.

As it came closer to train, they could tell it was a gigantic black cat. It ran toward their train car and collided with it. The lights flickered as the train was instantly derailed by the impact. All the passengers were violently thrown out of their seats. The cat pushed the train causing it to completely roll onto the highway adjacent to the tracks.

As the train stopped rolling, Melvin looked over at Denise who was unconscious and bleeding. He shook her trying to wake her up. Tears ran down his cheeks as he realized she was dead. He heard metal being ripped apart from above him. He looked up as a large black paw came down and grabbed him. As he was being lifted up, he could see the cat's sharp teeth getting closer. Within seconds, the cat swallowed him and then began grabbing as many passengers as it could to fill its belly.

Chapter Two

"Try it again," Benton shouted from the top of the thirty foot high robotic black cat. For the past year, his research team worked diligently to finish the Mecha Cat project. With the funding from the United States government and help from his team consisting of some of the brightest engineers in the field, Mecha Cat was going to be the top of the line defense against an enemy threat. Especially, if they were attacked by an over grown feline which his girlfriend, Lucille, and he encountered while they were lifeguarding at the Indiana Dunes National Lakeshore over two years ago.

"His head still won't move," Ajit Bahri, the lead engineer on the project, informed him. "There has to be something still not attached somewhere."

"Or it could be a software problem," Slater Malcrens, their computer software specialist, answered in disagreement.

"Whatever the problem is, we need to solve it," Benton stated as he climbed down the attached steps leading from its belly to its front left leg.

"Its front and rear paws are functional," Ajit said.

They watched as it moved forward a few feet. The room shook slightly with each step.

"Now that's impressive," Lucille said, walking into the lab. Her raven black hair was tied back in a ponytail, and she wore cutoff blue jeans and a tank top displaying her perfectly tanned body. "Aren't we supposed to be somewhere?"

"The party. I forgot."

Benton briefly looked over at her and then back at the schematic on his computer screen. His beach tanned body was gone since he quit being a lifeguard after the incident and locked himself in the lab designing and building Mecha Cat.

"Can we pass on it tonight?"

"Benton, the party was your idea. We haven't told any of our family about our engagement yet."

"Guys, you need to see the news," Lana Coast said as she ran into the lab. "There was an attack on the South Shore Line near the steel mill." She looked straight at Lucille. "A twenty foot black cat."

Slater turned on the large screen television, and they watched the horrific footage from the train wreckage.

Benton looked over at his team. "We need this thing fully operational, ASAP."

"We'll spend the whole night working out the remaining kinks," Ajit assured him.

"I'll contact Sergeant Alvarez and have his team rendezvous with me in Chesterton. Lucille, I'm sorry about the party."

"I know," she said sadly. "Be careful."

"I will. Notify me when Mecha Cat is operational."

He quickly gave her a kiss and rushed out of the lab.

Benton passed the entrance of the steel mill and pulled over to the side of the road where the police had the area barricaded off. The other side of the road was lined with vans from every news station in the area with reporters waiting for any new tidbit about the train accident.

"Let him through," Sergeant Alvarez said to one of the police officers as he saw Benton through the crowd of spectators.

"Did anybody see where it went?" Benton asked as he walked past the barricade.

Sergeant Alvarez was wearing a bluish camouflage uniform covered in fresh blood. "Witnesses saw it run into Lake Michigan and swim north. It left no survivors. The whole train is covered in blood. Be careful the ground is slippery."

Benton surveyed the wreckage and listened to the coroner describe the scene while the CSIs continued to collect evidence. Judging by the impressions on the ground, the cat had to be over twenty feet tall. He looked over at the sergeant.

"I don't like that look on your face," the sergeant said.

"We are dealing with a kitten."

"You're suggesting there may be more than just one."

"Unfortunately."

"What's the progress on Mecha?"

"Tomorrow hopefully." Benton didn't look convinced. He stared at the wreckage. "Unbelievable."

"My troops are mobilizing. The tanks and rocket launchers should be here within the hour."

"We are going to need them."

Chapter Three

Patti parked her car in one of the handicap spots in front of the Kmart in Chesterton. Rusty, her tiny Pug, looked at her with inquisitive eyes.

"Yes, I will bring you back a treat."

She got out of the car and with the help of her cane, walked toward the entrance. She could hear the "It's A Small World" theme coming from the mini ride to the left of the front door as a little kid enjoyed rocking back and forth on it. She walked in, grabbed a cart, and then headed to the back of the store where all of the romance novels were.

As she was inside Kmart shopping, Rusty was in the car trying to stay on the front seat as the ground shook violently. The sound of multiple car alarms going off was too much for Rusty's ears. The shaking stopped. Looking straight at Rusty through the window was an overgrown black cat. It licked its lips as it stared at him.

Rusty peed all over the seat in fear. The cat picked up the car and shook it violently causing Rusty to bounce around the car like he was a ball in a pinball machine. The cat, losing interest in the Pug, threw the car into the air.

Meanwhile, Patti looked at all of the chew toys in the pet food aisle. The little toy shaped like a duck amused her.

"I wonder if Rusty will like this one."

As she walked out of the pet food aisle, her car crashed through the ceiling and onto the floor behind her. The driver side door popped open and Rusty's carcass rolled out.

Chapter Four

Arris Wright sat at the head of the conference table watching Neil Lewis present his design for the new shopping mall they were planning.

Arris recently purchased some swampland near the new subdivision the city was developing outside of Chesterton, Indiana. He was warned about the dangers of building a shopping mall on swampland, but he was willing to take the risk since he was able to purchase the land cheap, because people were afraid to develop there due to the incident at the Indiana Dunes two years prior.

As Neil finished his presentation, Arris motioned to him to sit down.

"I believe everyone here is impressed with the design."

He looked toward the board members who were all nodding their heads in approval.

"I hope everybody understands the significance of this project. Chesterton has been reluctant to allow additional discount outlets built since the rich folks and I quote, 'don't want the riffraff that these stores attract.' Imagine a new Chesterton with a Goodwill, Target, Kohl's, Golden Corral and it's being developed by an African American," he explained with a big smile.

"Sir, what about the incident today?" Tammy Lemstrom asked.

"I've been assured that the cat menace will be taken care of immediately. Besides, this will cause Chesterton's real estate prices to drop even further. We will be able to purchase additional land at a cheaper rate."

"Sir, won't this cause people to shy away from the area."

"Trust me; this will cause Chesterton to become a tourist attraction. If we can acquire the carcass of one of these overgrown felines, we can display its skeleton on a monument in the parking lot of the shopping center. People will come far and wide to have a picture taken with it. In the process, they will shop at our stores. Trust me; this is a financial opportunity," Arris explained.

"How are we going to acquire one of these carcasses?" Tammy asked.

"The government spent a lot of money this past year developing a robotic defense system, Mecha Cat, to battle further feline threats. In return for an opportunity to acquire a feline carcass, I shared in the financial burdens of the project. Mecha Cat is en route to Chesterton as we speak."

Chapter Five

Benton was talking to Lucille on his smart phone as five tanks including a missile launcher pulled into the parking lot of the steel mill.

"The cavalry just arrived. What's the ETA on Mecha Cat?" Benton asked. "Good. I'll see you soon."

Sergeant Alvarez walked over to him followed by Lt. Marcus Moztem.

"Mecha Cat will be here within the hour," Benton reported.

"Our feline friend has been spotted down by Kmart," Marcus stated.

"We have multiple drones in the area. We should be able to track its movements. Once we have a location, we will strike," Sergeant Alvarez said.

"We will finally get a chance to test Mecha Cat in the field," Benton added. "I hope all my team's hard work pays off."

They almost lost their balance as the ground shook violently.

"Sir, we have a visual," Marcus reported.

Above the tree line across the street, they could see the tips of the cat's ears. Several frightened deer ran across the highway as the trees behind them crashed forward. The cat stopped as it reached the highway and stared at the several reporters and spectators who ran away. It chased after the deer toward the steel mill parking lot where the tanks were waiting.

"Fire!" Sergeant Alvarez shouted.

The missile launcher fired several missiles toward the cat that swatted them away with its paws sending the missiles into several directions. Several of the police cars exploded as the missiles collided with them. The tanks fired their projectiles doing minimum damage to the cat's body. The cat stared at the tanks angrily and rushed forward. As it collided with the lead tank, several soldiers fired at it from behind. The cat turned around and hissed at them. As its attention was focused on the soldiers, the tanks fired at it from close range. Wounded, the cat jumped over the soldiers and was forced to ground in midair by Mecha Cat.

The cat slowly stood up and hissed at Mecha Cat. It pounced onto it and Mecha Cat bit into its neck with its mechanical teeth. The cat used its momentum to roll sideways causing Mecha Cat and it to roll down the highway. The cat pulled itself away from Mecha Cat's grip and rammed it sending it backward a few feet. Mecha Cat ripped the cat's chest open with its left claw, causing it to spray blood all over the highway.

The cat quickly turned around, jumped over the soldiers and the tanks, and ran toward Lake Michigan. Mecha Cat chased after it as it jumped into the lake and swam north.

Benton's phone rang as Lucille called him from inside Mecha Cat.

"How are you holding up?" Benton asked.

"Would you call that a successful field test?" Lucille asked.

"You kicked its ass."

"You know it. Does Alvarez have any orders?"

Benton handed his phone over to the sergeant.

"That was impressive. Are you tracking it?" the sergeant asked.

"It's heading for Canada."

"Follow it back to its home. Kill it and any others. We need you to bring its body back."

"Understood."

He handed the phone back to Benton.

"Lucille, be careful."

"Benton, I will."

Lucille looked over at Slater who was sitting next to her. "Follow it."

"Following its course now."

As it entered Lake Michigan, it transformed into a submarine. It traveled in the same direction that the cat was swimming. As they moved forward, Slater spotted something huge swimming in the lake.

"What is that?" Lucille asked.

"I believe it's a shark," Slater answered.

They stared at it in shock. The shark was bigger than they had ever seen making a great white look minuscule. The shark began to glow bright yellow and vanished.

"Where did it go?" Lucille asked, amazed.

"It looked like it was transported like in the Star Trek movies," Slater pointed out.

"According to the readout, we are approaching Canada. Prepare to transform."

"Lucille, it's surfacing."

"Slater, follow it."

Mecha Cat climbed out of the lake and followed the trail of blood pouring from the cat's wound. They followed it down a hill toward a group of trees. Up ahead in a clearing were three other cats: a white one, a grey one and a calico. The black cat crashed to the ground near the other three and died.

"There's three more of them. What should we do?" Slater asked.

"Arm all our weapons and kill them all."

As the last of the three cats were killed, Mecha Cat walked over to them and picked the calico one up with its mouth to take back to Chesterton.

"I can't wait to get out of this thing. It's too cramped in here," Slater said, smiling.

"We did well."

Mecha Cat shook violently.

"I'm picking up something massive heading in our direction," Slater reported.

A large calico cat twice the size of the other four walked through the trees and stared at Mecha Cat angrily.

"That would be the mother," Lucille said in shock.

The cat ran forward slamming Mecha Cat into the ground. The cat ran behind a large tree and pushed it forward causing it to crash onto Mecha Cat's torso. Lucille messed with the controls trying to unpin it from the tree. Mecha Cat slowly pulled itself out from under the tree and was instantly slammed into another one by the angry feline.

"I think we are losing!" Slater shouted.

"Really!"

"I would suggest ramming it with all our might."

"It's worth a shot."

Mecha Cat ran forward and slammed the cat into a tree. The cat hissed exposing all its large teeth. Mecha Cat shot a missile toward it. The missile collided with its teeth shattering them. Mecha Cat rammed it again and ripped its neck open with its right claw. The cat stared at them and tried to lift its right paw, but it fell down limp as it died.

"Who's the boss? That's right us!" Slater chanted.

"Something's happening."

The cat glowed as its spirit left its body. The cat's ghost looked at them and floated forward.

"What the hell?" Slater screamed as the inside of Mecha Cat glowed bright red.

Mecha Cat screamed and spun around in a circle violently.

"What's going on?" Slater shouted holding on to his seat for dear life.

"I think its spirit has possessed Mecha Cat!"

Mecha Cat continued to scream and then ran toward Lake Michigan. It jumped into the lake and swam back toward Chesterton.

"Slater, I can't access its computer."

"It has complete control of navigation."

"If it has control of navigation, then it has control of the weapons systems. We need to disable them before it gets back to the States."

"On it."

Slater walked over to its computer core. As he opened the hatch, he was hit with a bolt of electricity sending his body violently backward. He hit his head against the panel next to Lucille knocking him unconscious. The panel adjacent to Lucille exploded, knocking her to the ground. As she was about to stand up, she was hit with a bolt of electricity knocking her unconscious, as well.

Benton and Sergeant Alvarez watched as Mecha Cat emerged from Lake Michigan. Benton sensed something was wrong when he noticed that Mecha Cat was mutated. Its eyes were no longer red, but looked more like real cat's eyes, the left one blue and the right one gold. It had fur growing out of its joints.

It hissed at them and then fired a missile.

"Take cover!" the sergeant shouted.

One of the tanks exploded on impact.

It walked toward them as it continued to hiss.

"What the hell is going on?" the sergeant asked.

"I think it's possessed," Benton answered.

"We need to destroy it."

"Lucille is inside."

"Do you have any suggestions?" the sergeant asked as Mecha Cat fired another missile destroying another tank.

"Keep it distracted. I'll climb the steps up its leg and enter through the hatch. I'll rescue Lucille and Slater and then drop a grenade into its computer core."

"Sounds dangerous and stupid," the sergeant said.

"That describes my personality perfectly."

"Good luck."

The sergeant handed him a grenade. He ran over to his troops and ordered them to attack. Benton ran toward Mecha Cat hoping his plan would succeed.

A chopper flew past Mecha Cat and fired a missile toward it. It deflected it with one of its paw and then pounced upward and caught the chopper in its mouth. It shook it violently and then flung the chopper into Lake Michigan.

Mecha Cat continued to deflect the missiles from the tanks as Benton began to climb up its left leg. As he reached its hatch, he grabbed onto the handle and was hit with an electrical shock. He quickly grabbed it again and turned the handle and opened the hatch. He jumped in and rolled out of the way of an electrical bolt. He rushed over to Lucille and tried to shake her awake. She moaned painfully as she regained consciousness. He turned his attention to Slater and shook him awake.

"Don't open the hatch to the computer core," he warned. "Electric shock."

"Take off your jacket. When I throw this grenade in the computer core, I need you two to jump out the hatch. It's a long jump, but a couple of broken bones is better than being blown to shreds," Benton said. "Can you guys stand?"

"I'll try," Lucille said as she slowly stood up.

"Get ready."

Benton wrapped his left hand with Slater's jacket and lifted the hatch to the computer core. He pulled the pin and dropped the grenade into the computer core as Slater and Lucille jumped out. He turned around and quickly jumped out of Mecha Cat as the grenade went off.

Mecha Cat screamed loudly as its internal systems exploded. A few seconds later, its head exploded sending fire and debris into every direction.

As Lucille was standing up from the jump, a small piece of debris landed on her right arm. Her arm glowed a bright white for a few seconds. She felt dizzy and passed out.

Her eyes opened and she was lying on a bed at Porter Memorial Hospital. She looked over at Benton, Slater, and Ajit who were discussing the events of the past couple of days.

"Pay no attention to me," she said with a smile. "Do I look as bad as I feel?"

"You have a concussion and a few fractured bones. Otherwise, as beautiful as ever," Benton answered.

"Thanks, I think. Is it over?"

"Yes, there is no more feline threats," Slater answered.

"That we know of," Ajit added.

"Promise me we are done with this. I want to have a normal life," Lucille said.

"Benton, you better tell her," Ajit said.

"Tell me what?"

"The government wants us to begin construction of another Mecha Cat right away," Benton answered and all three of them began laughing. "Believe me, I think the last thing they will want is for us to build another one."

"I hope so for all our sakes," she said with a smile.

Chapter Six

"Arris, it is this way," the man in the black uniform said as he led him down the corridor leading to the large hangar outside the secret government base in Nevada.

As they entered the corridor, Arris stood in amazement at the sight before him. Inside a large electrified steel cage was a twenty foot white cat with dark green eyes. It stared at him as he approached the cage.

"Hello, my feline friend."

"This is the father. We found the bodies of the mother and the four kittens in Canada."

"Will you provide me with the mother's skeleton as promised?" Arris asked.

"Do you have what we requested?"

"It took a lot of effort to secure them. As I promised you over the phone, here's the blueprints for Mecha Cat." Arris answered and handed him a thumb drive with the plans.

"You need to keep this a secret."

"Trust me; as long as I get the skeleton, you get my silence."

"I will have the skeleton transported to wherever you want."

"Thanks."

Arris stared at the cat. It hissed at him and rammed into the cage violently and jumped backward as it was shocked by the electric cage. It sat down, stared at him for a few seconds, then closed its eyes and went to sleep.

Chapter Seven

Lucille climbed out of bed. She was burning up and she knew if she didn't get to the bathroom soon, she would be throwing up all over the floor. She rushed into the bathroom and began to throw up. She held onto the sink to avoid losing balance since she felt dizzy.

As her body temperature cooled down, she began to feel like her whole body was itchy. She looked down and her whole body was covered in black fur. She tried to scream as she looked in the mirror, but no sound would come out. Standing before her was not the beautiful tanned brunette woman that she knew, but a feline humanoid with black fur and glowing yellow eyes. She looked at her hands and her fingernails were eight inches long.

She hissed at her reflection and ran out of the bathroom toward the bedroom. She rushed over to her bed to wake Benton up. She slowly walked backward in horror. In the middle of the bed lay Benton covered in blood. His body was ripped apart and in the middle of his chest lay three kittens asleep. She felt something rubbing against her legs and looked down to see a calico cat. She picked it up and it purred as she held it in her arms.

Rastus, A Warrior's Quest

Rastus stared at the skeletons littering the forest floor. Beside each bleached-bone body lay their swords; all damaged from exposure to the elements. These were the fallen men of his tribe, Klytrinx of the Forest. They had failed to succeed in their spiritual passage from adolescence to manhood. Rastus, himself on the brink of manhood, blinked back his tears when he recognized the sword next to one of the skeletons. It belonged to Dashiell, his best friend, and the last tribesman to leave the village and go on the great spiritual journey. Only half of the tribesman who ventured out ever returned. Those who came home, never spoke of the journey. It was a rite of passage for the men of the woods. He had watched the boys leave every year, and knew the 'ritual to manhood' was a death sentence only the strongest could survive. This was why he constantly trained in the physical arts. His large muscular physique was the result.

He picked up Dashiell's sword and compared it to his own. It was a fine sword: the hilt had symbols etched into it and the blade was still sharp. The sword of Rastus was adorned with three shiny, red rubies he'd found some time ago. He respectfully replaced Dashiell's sword next to his skeleton. The bones along his friend's rib cage, around his heart, were crushed. Something large had penetrated Dashiell's chest. Rastus would have to be very cautious. Whatever evil had happened; it had taken the lives of his tribesmen.

The forest emitted no sound, as if the animals and insects suspected danger. Rastus surveyed the area around him, but didn't see anything of immediate threat. As he checked the ground, he recalled his last meeting with his grandfather, Kotori.

They were sitting by the fire admiring the moonlight from the clear night sky. Kotori was preparing him for the spiritual journey.

"You must become one with nature. You must not fear nature, but rather, embrace it with all its good and bad."

"What should I expect?"

"Rastus, the spirits will test your worthiness. If they deem you unworthy for this world, you will not survive the journey. I cannot tell you any more."

Rastus had long contemplated why his people had to prove their merit to the spirits. So many of his tribesmen tried and failed. He didn't want to be the next one who couldn't succeed. He valued life, not only his own but all around him.

He froze, craning his neck toward the sudden sound that sent a chill down his spine. At first, the sound was faint but as it drew closer, he could hear loud pounding. The ground shook as the sound drew near. Whatever it was, it was huge. A tree in front of him fell, snapping at its base. An enormous grey creature with long tusks stood before him. His grandfather had once described such a creature. A mammoth.

He gripped his sword tightly, anticipating an attack. The giant stared at him; anger in its body language.

The bushes shook as a large black bear walked through. It stood next to the mammoth, staring straight at Rastus. Despite all his physical training, Rastus knew he was no match against the animals.

He heard a roar, and seconds later a huge saber-toothed tiger appeared. The three beasts stepped forward, threateningly.

It was obvious that any move against these creatures would be a death sentence. All he could do was drop his sword. He raised his hands in surrender.

"My name is Rastus and I mean you no harm."

The mammoth lowered its head.

The other two beasts vanished.

The mammoth glowed a fire bright orange and transformed into a tall, beautiful woman in a vibrant yellow garb with flowing auburn hair. Rastus had never seen anyone so beautiful before. She was not part of his tribe; nor did she look like anyone from any neighboring tribes.

"My name is Alzina. I welcome you to my forest. As you can tell from the ground around you, most men choose to attack. You chose to drop your sword."

"There is no sense in fighting a losing battle."

"Wise."

She walked over to him and ran her hand across his muscular physique and stopped over his heart. Her hand felt cold against his chest. She smiled as she slowly walked away. "Follow."

He stared at her as she disappeared into the deep forest.

"Follow."

He heard her voice echo. He walked forward through the thick trees. She was nowhere in sight, but he could hear the sound of her voice echoing in the forest, urging him forward. He came upon a clearing that opened onto a large waterfall. Alzina sat atop a large moss covered stone. She played a silver harp. She motioned for him to sit on the ground in front of the stone. A fox jumped onto the stone and stretched out next to her.

"This place is peaceful," Rastus said as a rainbow colored butterfly landed on his shoulder.

"This is a place of magic."

She placed the harp on her lap and snapped her fingers. The waterfall disappeared, exposing a large cave.

"You have two choices. You can turn back, return to your village and claim your spiritual journey complete; or you can venture into the cave to prove your worthiness."

"Worthiness for what?"

"To be the protector of life. To be the protector of this sacred forest."

"Protector from what?"

"The biggest threat to my animals and to my forest."

"Which is?"

"Mankind," she said sadly.

"Mankind respects nature."

"Unfortunately not for long. One day mankind will want to venture further into the world. Progress they will call it. First the forests will disappear, then the animals, and then mankind. I need someone; a gentle soul and a warrior all in one; who can protect what I've worked so hard for my whole existence to protect."

"Am I the first to be worthy?"

"There have been a few others, but they chose to return to your tribe instead of staying on as protector. Only one chose to be my champion."

"What happened to him?"

"He died many years ago. He was my champion for a long time."

"How long?"

"Longer than you could possibly imagine."

"If I take the offer, what do I get in return?"

"You will be blessed by the gods and have fortunes beyond your wildest imagination in the afterlife."

He stared at her for a few seconds and then at the cave. Alzina began to play her harp as she waited for his decision. A lion ambled over to him and sat down at his feet. He had never been close to one before and was amazed the lion wasn't a threat.

"Animals are friends to my kind and they will be to you if you accept my offer," she said as she played on.

He cautiously put his left hand on the lion and began to pet it. The lion slowly looked up at him and yawned. Rastus laughed in disbelief. He looked over at Alzina and smiled.

"Enter the cave and become my champion."

He walked into the cave. There were glowing blue diamonds along the walls brightening up the passageway. Carved into the wall were depictions of a muscular man wielding a sword, surrounded by wild animals. He stopped for a few minutes to admire the carvings before venturing further into the cave. At the end of the passageway was a large boulder that was flat on top with an outline of a sword etched into it. Taking out his sword, Rastus placed it on the outline. It began to glow bright red and then vanished, reappearing a few seconds later. What once was a silver sword was now gold. He picked up the weapon admiring its new beauty.

"You alone are the wielder of this magic sword, as long as you follow an honest path. Follow a dark path and it will turn on you," Alzina warned.

"What do I do now?"

"Venture forward into the world. What lies ahead is nothing compared to what you've encountered so far. There is a different world beyond the forest. Listen to the animals. They will be your guides. Until we meet again."

Alzina vanished.

He re-placed his sword in the familiar leather-bound scabbard, suspended from the strap across his right shoulder. He followed the passageway out of the cave. The forest looked very different. The leaves on the trees were colored red and orange and the ground was littered with the fallen leaves. When he entered the cave it had been spring and now it seemed to be fall.

How long had he been in the cave?

Next to the cave entrance there were markings carved in a large stone. These were ancient symbols his grandfather taught him to read. Cave of Time. It didn't have a meaning to him for now. He changed direction to his village. He reached the end of the forest where he had learned to swim in. A canoe he'd left tied to a rock was nowhere in sight. He jumped into the water and swam across. On the other side, he sat down and rested. He had a couple of hours of daylight left, so he grabbed some sticks and a couple of rocks and built a fire. The sun disappeared and he watched the stars before falling asleep.

The sound of something splashing in the water awoke him. He opened his eyes to find a saber-toothed tiger asleep at his feet. A large, multi-colored fish repeatedly jumped in the river. On the other side of the river were four beautiful white horses, each with a golden horn on the top of its head. He had never seen anything like them before.

The tiger raised its head and stared at him. As Rastus stood up, so did the tiger.

"What's wrong?"

The tiger ran for the forest, stopped and stared at him.

"You want me to follow?"

Rastus pulled his sword out of the scabbard and followed the tiger into the forest. He could hear the sound of a large animal struggling up ahead. As he drew closer, he heard somebody ordering to attack. He saw a mammoth in the distance. Three men in brown leather armor had a rope tied around one of its tusks.

"Subdue the beast! His tusks will make great weapons!" their leader yelled out.

Two men wrapped a rope on the same tusk and pulled, trying to force the mammoth to the ground. Rastus jumped forward and sliced one of the ropes with his sword. He violently pushed three of the men backward with his left hand.

"Kill him!" their leader commanded.

Rastus cut the other rope. The men carried carved wooden clubs, long and heavy. One young man swung at him. Rastus deflected the blow with his leather armor on his left forearm and swung his sword with his right, slicing the club in half. Another man rushed at him while the third unsuccessfully tried to stop the mammoth from escaping.

Their leader watched the fight in awe. His men's clubs were no match for the strength of Rastus's sword.

"I want his weapon! Take it from him!"

Rastus fought the group of three until each of them lay on the ground unconscious. Their leader began to run away, then stopped, and turned around and stared at him. He knew he didn't stand a chance against a warrior like Rastus.

"Who are you?"

"Rastus, protector of the animals."

"Another time, Rastus." He nodded his head in respect and walked away.

Rastus lowered his sword and looked at the tiger who was standing over the men ready to attack if they regained consciousness.

"We better go before they wake up. My village is not far from here."

The tiger followed him. They reached the end of the forest and entered a clearing. Rastus stared in disbelief. His village was in ruins. All that remained was the large well that used to be the center of the village.

"Your people have been gone for a long time," Alzina said from behind him.

"What happened?"

"This village was one of many destroyed by the Zentlox."

"Where are these Zentlox?"

"Like your people; they were conquered. You've been away from this land for hundreds of years."

"Why am I in the future?"

"Because this is the time when my forest and the animals need you most. This will be your first test, your first journey. Return the balance between nature and mankind."

"If I fail?"

Alzina's eyes turned a dark red. "Do not fail!" Her eyes returned to their natural shade of blue. "If you fail, my animals will disappear from this world one by one."

Rastus looked over at the tiger licking its left paw and then back at Alzina.

"I won't fail. This I promise you."

"Your quest begins north," Alzina said and disappeared.

He could see a large mountain off to the north. He walked past the well and into the forest on the other side with the tiger following behind him. He looked back at what was once his village with sadness. He thought about his parents, his grandfather and the other people of his tribe. He had outlived them all. He said a prayer and continued to walk forward.

Alzina watched him from a distance.

"He has a strong heart which sickens me, but even strong hearts can be broken," a large, muscular, red-skinned creature with a head similar to a lion said as he appeared next to her. He was a demon from the underworld who despised nature and wanted mankind to destroy it.

"Tyles, I have faith in him. He will succeed."

"We shall see," he said as he sat down next to her. "He's heading for my land. You know I will have to stop him."

"He will defeat you."

"Maybe, maybe not. Alzina, to my victory," Tyles said arrogantly and disappeared.

"Arrogance will be your downfall."

The End

The adventures of Rastus will continue in the novel "Beast Within" by Derek Ailes coming in 2016.

SHELANA'S QUEST

Shelana stared out the window of her hut watching a unicorn drinking out of the pond by the large tree. It was beautiful with its white fur and the golden horn on its head. She didn't want to venture outside because she was afraid she would startle it into running away. Her sister, Melody, walked over to her curious about what had caught her attention.

"She's magnificent," Melody said while braiding her long, black hair. Once finished, she put her hands on Shelana's reddish hair.

"I don't want my hair tied up today," Shelana said as she moved her hair away from her.

"You have the most beautiful hair in the world. Why must you go about with it so messy?"

"Melody, I love the way it flows in the wind."

"You are a warrior, remember?"

"Just because I'm an elf, doesn't mean I have to be a warrior," she said, pointing at her pointed ears.

"Even warriors must look their best. We never know who we will encounter."

"Hoping to find an elf prince? Not too many venture this far into the forest. At least, I have never seen one here."

"Shelana, you never know."

"Face it, we are isolated out here as the guardians of the forest. Our only friends are the animals and the butterflies. Occasionally, we encounter a fairy, but that's it."

"Shelana, your unicorn just ran away. Want to go outside where that wind of yours is?"

She moved her hand toward her hair again.

"Melody, stop!"

"I'm just playing with you," she said with a big smile. "The last one out must kiss a frog."

"Probably turn me into a frog instead."

Shelana walked over to the pond and admired her reflection. The wind caused her hair to flow backward. The sound of the birds chirping calmed her.

Melody walked over to her holding something hidden in her hand. "I found your frog prince."

"Put him down."

"Fine. That's probably the only chance you'll…"

A tiger roared in the distance.

"There's danger nearby," Shelana said as she ran into the hut to retrieve her bow and arrow. Melody followed her and grabbed her sword.

The tiger continued to roar.

"Sounds like it's coming from the middle of the forest. Melody, prepare yourself."

"I'm always prepared."

They ventured farther into the forest. The only sounds they heard was from the tiger warning them of imminent danger.

"Do you smell that? Could it be?"

"Shelana, I can smell something rotten. Definitely a reptilian. I suggest an aerial assault."

Melody climbed a thick, green vine up the side of the nearest tree. Once she was at the top, Shelana grabbed the vine and climbed. Melody grabbed another vine and swung across and landed on a large branch of the tree several feet away. Shelana waited for the vine to return and then swung across.

Melody pointed at Shelana's hair. "Maybe you should have let me tie it."

"I wasn't expecting to be tree hopping today. Can you see anything?"

"Not from here."

Melody grabbed another vine and swung over to another tree. She released the vine and kneeled down on the large branch and surveyed the forest below. She could see the tiger locked in a large wooden cage surrounded by several reptilian warriors. They were all dressed in thick metal armor with helmets aligned with animal bones. Their leader stood taller than the rest and, unlike the skinny, grey skeletal appearance of the other reptilians, was muscular. He held a large club made out of an elephant's ivory tusk.

"How many?" Shelana asked as she landed on the branch.

"I see eight including their leader."

"What do they want with the tiger?"

"Whatever the reason, it can't be good." Melody grabbed a dagger from her left leather boot. "Prepare for battle."

She threw the dagger and it embedded itself into one of the reptilian's necks. It fell forward dead.

"Who threw that? Show yourselves!" the reptilian leader commanded.

"Take out the smaller ones and I'll get their leader," Melody ordered.

She grabbed a vine and swung toward the leader. He deflected her sword attack with his club causing her to lose her grip on the vine. She fell to the ground hard.

"An attack from a girl! Now that's hilarious!"

The leader swung his club toward her. She rolled out of the way avoiding its impact.

Three of the reptilians fell dead from Shelana's arrows.

Melody jumped up from the ground and swung her sword toward the leader who deflected it with his club. The other three remaining reptilians fell dead from Shelana's arrow attack.

"Give up. All your friend's are dead," Melody ordered.

"Never. Your sword is no match for my club."

As he held the club upward, an arrow penetrated his hand causing him to drop it. Melody swung her sword across his neck. He grabbed his neck as he fell to the ground. She pulled his helmet off and swung her sword downward slicing his head off.

Shelana swung down from the tree and landed on her feet. She walked over to the wooden cage and released the tiger. It stared at her as she put her hand on its head.

"You are free now."

It raised its head in acknowledgment and walked away.

"Thank you for saving my tiger," a voice from behind them said.

They both turned around startled. Standing before them was a tall female with long, flowing, red hair dressed in a glowing yellow garb. She held a silver harp in her hand that played without her plucking any strings.

"Who are you?" Shelana asked.

"My name is Alzina."

"My name is Shelana and this is my sister, Melody. We are the guardians of this forest. How come we have never encountered you before?"

"I've never had a reason to reveal myself to you until now. The world is changing. The reptilians are advancing farther into the forest and extinction now faces my animals. As you can see from the animal bones aligning their armor and the club made from one of my elephant's ivory tusks, how much of a threat they are. As their numbers grow, my animals diminish. This has to stop before it's too late. I may be one of great magic, but my magic is useless to the animals that have perished. I can heal those that are injured, but it is forbidden for me to use my magic to resurrect the dead."

"How can we help?" Shelana asked.

"There is a magic crystal which can save my forest. Find it and place it on top of the oldest tree in the forest. Once the task is completed, the reptilians will never be able to venture in here again."

"What about the animals that don't live in the forest?" Melody asked.

"There is another chosen for that task. A warrior named Rastus. Your task is protection of this forest. Find the magic crystal for me. There is an artifact hidden in the ancient ruins of Klytrinxs that will guide you on your quest."

Alzina vanished. Melody stared at Shelana in shock.

"We better head back home to pack supplies. We have a long journey ahead of us," Shelana advised.

"Klytrinxs. I heard legends about that place. They say a great warrior was born there centuries ago, but still lives."

"He was the warrior she was talking about."

"So the legend is true."

"I hope all of the legends about Klytrinxs aren't true."

"Shelana, why not?"

"They say the place is guarded by a monster. One that can't be killed."

The adventures of Shelana and Melody will continue in the novel "Beast Within" by Derek Ailes coming in 2016.

The Stories Behind The Demented Mind

I hope everyone enjoyed the musings from the demented minds of James Coon and me, Derek Ailes. I was sitting in the office at work when I found out about JC's passing. Even though no autopsy was performed, his death was ruled complications from diabetes. Five days later, I met with his sister, Linda, and his niece, Amber. I asked them if they could locate a couple of notebooks filled with stories he had been writing from the 1990's until a week before he passed away. To my surprise, not only did they find the two notebooks; they found his whole school writing file that included stories going all the way back to the 1960s.

I had already decided minutes after finding out about his passing that I was going to write a collection of short stories based on all of the conversations we've had over the past fifteen years. He had a lot of interesting stories to tell. I wanted to include his story "Sirens of Lake Station" and I wanted to finish the story he started a week before — "Travelers". With receiving his writing file, I found several other stories that I decided to also include in this anthology. There are a lot more stories of his in the file, but these were the ones that fit this anthology perfectly.

Here's a little background on James Coon:

He was born on July 5, 1952 in Connersville, Indiana to Lloyd Coon & Mary Phyllis Teller. He was preceded in death by his parents and infant brother, Danny.

He graduated from Wheeler High School in 1972. He had been working overnights in the produce department of Strack & Van Til and Wiseway Foods in

Valparaiso, IN for twenty years and had previously served as an insurance representative. He enjoyed bowling in leagues, but relished the challenge of searching genealogy records. He was a diehard White Sox fan. He was a serious reader and I mean serious reader. Everywhere you turned in his house were stacks and stacks of books. He loved mysteries, science fiction and books on haunted houses and alien abductions. He was also one of the biggest DC comic book fans I have ever met. He spent a lot of time at Galactic Greg's Comic Book Shop along with Barnes & Noble in Valparaiso, IN. He would have me order numerous books through Amazon for him on a regular basis. Back when I used to sell used books on eBay, he would give me a long list of books to look for him when I was out hunting the resale shops for rare and out of print books.

His father would take him to the movies when he was a child and that is where his love for classic movies began. Film noir was one of his favorite movie styles. We would sit for hours discussing all the movie classics, and he would tell me about all the behind the scenes details of each film he watched. http://www.imdb.com was one of his favorite websites, and he would visit the website after watching each film. When he was in the retirement home, he would watch all the classics on Turner Classic Movies. I was always amazed at how he could recite every little detail about each movie. I gained a new respect for the classics over the years thanks to him, and my classic movie DVD collection has been steadily growing ever since.

JC went to a school for the hearing impaired where he learned to read lips and to use sign language. He was misunderstood by most people and they never realized how brilliant he really was. It wasn't until I began reading all of his writings that I realized he was more brilliant than I ever realized. Then again, we are talking about a guy who would read anything he got his hands on. In the months he was in the nursing home, he read over forty books.

    His ability to read lips came in handy at work. I heard a lot of interesting tidbits about my co-workers from when he read their lips when they were gossiping back and forth.

    He had been living at his mother's house all of his life and inherited it several years back after her death. He was a very private man and only a select few of us had the honor of being a part of his social circle.

    I first met him in 1999 when I started working at Wiseway Foods. I would work as the dairy assistant and on Sundays I would also sweep and mop the floors since my buddy, Jim Butler, would be off that night. I would go over to produce, mop the floors, and talk with JC. We immediately hit it off thanks to both of our love of the Beatles. Neither of us took George Harrison's death too well. JC and I were both comic book geeks and avid readers. We had endless amount of things we could talk about and JC found it easier to talk to me about his personal life than anyone he knew.

    JC and I would talk for hours about music, haunted houses, alien abductions, his experiences with haunted houses and cemeteries, his family and his genealogy research. After my brother, Mark Cusco Ailes, published his first book, JC brought me a yellow notebook that had his story "Sirens of Lake Station" in it and told me he wanted to one day write a whole novel out of it. He also told me several story ideas he had and, luckily for this anthology, he went into detail on how the stories would go.

Over the years, we had many adventures playing tricks on unsuspecting co-workers, our late friend, Jim Hampson, being one of the main ones. I remember one time, Hampson was in produce mopping the floors and JC ran to his CD player and put a Native American Chanting CD on. The moment the CD started, Hampson jumped back in fear. We never laughed so hard after watching Hampson almost hit the ceiling because he jumped so high.

JC and Jim Butler, (we just called him Butler at work. There was a time when we had five Jims working at Wiseway and that is why we called everybody by nicknames) possessed a strange relationship. JC would go out of his way to antagonize him on a nightly basis. Besides the normal arguing with him over comic book trivia and which was better DC or Marvel (Marvel in my opinion, but I like both), JC would wait for Butler to bring his scrubber into his department to clean the floors, and he would deliberately move things into his path. I spent way too much time refereeing the two of them. Butler knew he was doing it on purpose.

JC's health had always been poor. His diabetes was way out of control and one of his legs was so black from the diabetes that his doctor wanted to have it amputated. JC was a very stubborn individual and didn't want to have his leg amputated. He searched for a doctor until he found one that was willing to treat his diabetes without an amputation being an option. This was a mistake he lived to regret for years to come. After having a heart attack two years back, his health was on a downward spiral until he ended up in the hospital and his current doctor told him that if he didn't have the leg amputated, he would be dead within a month.

Finally, he had the amputation which he should have had decades before. He ended up in a retirement and rehabilitation center. He was fitted for a prosthetic leg. Once he was released from the retirement center, he went back to work. He was healthier and moved around with a speed and determination that I had not seen before. He had major plans for 2015. He was going to officially retire this summer and finally write a book. I told him if he wrote the book, I would make sure it would get published. He began writing "Travelers". The Saturday before he passed, he brought me the first page to see what my opinion of it was. He wanted to write the book and then have a comic book made out of it, as well. He was no longer saying he would write and publish someday; he was serious now. I don't know if it had to do with the fact I had three published books by that time and was planning a fourth one, but he wanted to see his name on a book.

It does sadden me to think that this didn't happen until after his passing. This whole project is me keeping a promise to help him get published and show the world the side of him no one else had a chance to see.

Part of this project is me saying goodbye to a friend in a way only I can do.

Before meeting with his family, I began writing the first story for this anthology at the time titled "James Coon Ebook". I had a lot of stories to tell. This section is a sneak peek into the stories behind the stories. I will try to explain the true stories that go along with each of the stories. There are details of his life spread out throughout the first part of the anthology.

Let's Begin.

Yes, Mother!: This story is based on an experience JC had in his house after his mother had passed away. JC claimed to be able to sense spirits who hadn't passed on. He believed he could still sense his mother's presence in the house. One night while he was sleeping, he felt something heavy pushing down on his chest. When he awoke, he was paralyzed and a black spirit was hovering over his bed. When the spirit vanished, he was able to move around. He claimed that the spirit was of his mother.

I described his house in the story with the stacks of books all over the place. Potatoes were his favorite food, and I thought it was fitting that he would be eating one in the story.

Golden Age Retirement and Rehabilitation Center: This is based on his time he was recovering from his amputation. I visited him several times during his stay and witnessed a lot of things while I was there. Twilight Zone was one of his favorite shows and the Roddy McDowell episode was one of his favorite episodes. JC had several prescriptions and carried a bag with him everywhere filled with them and several books. He would always have me bring him Lipton Ice Tea and butter flavored microwave popcorn. One day when I was there, the person in the bed next to him stopped breathing and the nurses and doctor rushed in. He was taken away by ambulance.

The two nurses in the story, Breanne and Christine, are the names of two African American women who he knew from Gary. He always claimed Christine was his daughter and Breanne was his granddaughter. His sister and family talked to Christine and she denied it. She said they were just friends, and she would help him out when she could.

Kenner is based on one of the patients there who sat in his wheelchair in the hallway and waited for anyone to pass him so he could start a conversation. I bumped into him and his wife a few weeks back at the Goodwill in Portage. While he was looking at the DVDs, I talked with his wife. She would pick him up, take him out for a while, and then take him back to the nursing home. He really is a nice guy.

During the time JC stayed there, a patient walked out the back door after one of the nurses forgot to lock it. The patient was found walking down the middle of Willowcreek Rd by the police.

A severe storm hit the Portage area during his stay. A large branch snapped off the top of the tree behind my house. It landed on my car and my truck. Luckily it only did minor damage to both of my vehicles. My car was in perfect condition before that. Ironically, a few weeks later we were leaving JC's house. He has a telephone pole right there adjacent to the very narrow driveway on the right. There is a tree where branches have overgrown over the driveway that made it impossible to see pulling out of the driveway. I went into reverse and my passenger side mirror hit the telephone poll. Smack! Now the mirror is permanently wrapped in black duct tape. I refer to it as the result of one of my adventures with JC.

You can tell from the story that JC had a strange sense of humor. Even when he felt his worst, he couldn't pass up on playing a joke or being sarcastic.

There are elements from the movies "Cocoon", "Invasion of the Body Snatchers" and "Alien" in this story.

Sirens of Lake Station: This was written by JC sometime in the 1990s. I took the original story and modernized it. Scott Drugs was the original store in the story, but they went out of business a long time ago. This was the story I wanted to get my hands on. I wanted people to have a chance to read this one. This is my favorite of all his stories. I'm glad his sister was able to find it.

Alien Town: This story is my tribute to JC's obsession with alien encounters and abductions. Alice and Tara are the names of two Russian porn stars who came to the United States to meet up with American men who JC would correspond with back and forth on the internet. He actually went to Chicago to meet them in person. While they were in California they had a problem with someone (let's call him a fan) getting out of hand and Alice had to pull a gun out on him. The backstory of them witnessing the Russian mob killing some of their clients, is based on a story JC told me about. I used both of these incidents as inspiration to write this story.

The name of the gas station is Superman's father and the names of the police officers are variations of different DC comic book characters. Dean, obviously based on JC, is named after Dean Koontz. Being clairvoyant is a theme throughout some of these stories. JC claimed to have this ability and it was also the theme throughout a lot of the stories in his writing file.

Haunted Attractions: One day while doing his genealogical research, JC was at a cemetery photographing the tombstone of one of his ancestors. After having the pictures developed, yes this was before digital cameras became the norm, he discovered that he had photographed an image of a ghost in the corner of each of the images. People argued with him saying there must have been a flaw in the film. He believed it was in fact a ghost. All the pictures before the cemetery and after on the roll came out with no suspicious white image in the corner. This story was about that day in the cemetery. People familiar with haunted houses in Indiana and throughout America will know what house in Gary I am referring to. There was an article in a British magazine about *the unexplained* published a couple years back about that house in Gary, IN.

Little Town Flirt: Originally titled "Madness Within Our Minds" was written by JC back in the 1970s. I came up with the new title after hearing the song by Del Shannon on the overhead radio at work. I had to change the ending since the last page of the story was missing. I have no idea how the original story ended. I decided to go with a "Tales From the Crypt" style ending.

Master of Discontent: The story was written by JC and was originally published in the Wheeler School Newspaper in 1971. This version includes the original last paragraph that was omitted from the version published by the school newspaper. The story is about suicide.

The Kick: This story was inspired by an encounter JC talked about from his childhood. I heard the story on several occasions over the years and thought a circus was the perfect setting to tell the story.

Games: This one was written by JC. The story is about the moral decline of society and how religion is important for our souls. This is a toned down version of the original story. This story dates back several decades.

Where Evil Shall Dwell: This was written by JC back in the 1970s. This was one of the stories that was a challenge for me to update. JC always wrote in first person, and I find that a challenge to write since I only write in third person. The story was his take on the mystery of the Bermuda triangle. This isn't the only story of JC's that Ira was in. The other story is an unfinished alien invasion story that one day I will go back and finish.

The Dogs: Originally titled "Night of The Dogs" was written by James Coon and me. I took the original story up to a certain point and I refuse to acknowledge the last few pages of that story exists. The story went in a direction I will never go. I have a list of a few topics I won't deal with in my writings and two of them were main components of the rest of the story. I reworked it with the lady actually turning into a dog. I had to rework some parts of the beginning scene since the main character actually does things that is a contradiction to the character JC had established. This story went through a lot of rewrites. I had the toughest time trying to fix this one, but I believed it was one that had to be included in this anthology.

Travelers: This was the story JC started working on a week before he passed away. The Saturday night before, he showed me the first page which sadly was the only page he finished. I took the first page and wrote it in the direction I thought he would have gone in. I spent a lot of time trying to make this story right. I hope he would have been proud of how it turned out. The first two pages of the story is from the one page he wrote.

When JC worked for the insurance company he won a trip to Russia. He often talked about his experiences there. I would say that trip was one of the favorite highlights of his life. JC liked a great bargain. He would buy a lot of clothes, mainly sweaters and flannel, at the Goodwill. With the amount of money he spent on comic books and paperbacks, he had to save the money somewhere. With his fascination with aliens, I thought it would be fitting to have part of the story take place in Area 51.

Agent Rick Venable and Agent Marilyn Austin are not modeled after Mulder and Scully from "X-Files". They are actually modeled after Phil Coulson and Melinda May from "Agents of S.H.I.E.L.D." The first time we encounter them was not in the original draft of the story. I was actually asleep when the idea of adding them to the story popped in my head. I snapped awake and immediately wrote the scene where they were in the park in Valparaiso. I compose my best stories while I'm sleeping. I reworked the parts I had already written to include those characters and how they affected the outcome of the story. In the original version of "Alien Town", Rick and Marilyn were in the ending. I decided weeks later that the scene didn't work and deleted it.

Yes, I had to mention the Beatles in one of my stories. The Beatles will stand the test of time. The White Album, in my opinion, is their best album and had the most mature song writing.

Reading the story with fresh eyes, I believe it turned out the way I was hoping. Maybe one day I will bring the characters back for another story. I promise you that we haven't seen the last of Agent Rick Venable and Agent Marilyn Austin.

"Travelers" closes the James Coon section of the anthology. I have plenty of his stories still to work through and someday I will publish some more of them. I hope everybody learned a lot about the man and enjoyed the journey through his demented mind.

For the musings from my mind.

I began working on stories for a new anthology back in December of last year. "Musings From the Demented Mind" was going to be the title for that anthology. I wrote "Lumps of Coal" and published it on Short Fiction Break in time for Christmas. I began working on several stories, but I went through a major non writing phase, writers' block. I decided I was going to begin writing my first full length novel "Beast Within". Short Fiction Break's first year anniversary was coming up and Jeff wanted to publish a new anthology of previous unpublished short stories by us SFB authors dealing with the concept for the first time, becoming one or anything dealing with the number one. I wrote my story "Rastus" to be included in the anthology. I was about to begin writing the first chapter of "Beast Within" when James Coon passed away. From there, my inspiration took off and I began writing religiously.

These stories prove that I have a demented mind.

Buzz Kill: The original idea for this story dates back to the "Zombie Command: A Horror Anthology" sessions. I came up with the idea from reading an article about a family who had a guest room they hadn't used in years. They had somebody who was going to stay with them and when they went in to prepare the room for her arrival, discovered thousands of bees had made a hive out of the mattress in the room. I came up with the idea that a girl was kidnapped and placed in a cellar. Bees entered the cellar and made a nest out of her. The outline was one of hundreds of outlines I came up with that I never did anything with. When the recent incident of the truck getting in the wreck on the highway unleashing millions of bees, I thought I now had an element to make my original idea work. I began writing it.

The main characters are based on people I know from work. Anybody who has read "The Freegans" from "Journey Into the Unknown: Deluxe Horror Edition" will get the reference when Julianne sees the guy digging through the dumpster in the back of the store.

This story is dedicated to all those who fear and are allergic to bees.

A Horror Story: This is a behind the scenes of making a low budget horror film. This is also a tribute to the movie "Waxwork". This story was originally written for Short Fiction Break. There are a lot of scenes inspired by several horror films throughout the story. This was one of those stories that I had a lot of fun writing.

Lumps of Coal: This one was written for Short Fiction Break for Christmas 2014. This is all about the top 1% of our country and what they think of us. It's all about greed. I will leave it to everyone's imagination who the rich snob was based on.

Elvis Has Left the Dead: Mark Cusco Ailes and I were interviewed for the Times newspaper recently. A photographer was sent to our book signing three days later to take a photograph of us for the article. Sandra had her Elvis cutout promoting her Elvis book standing up by the entrance to the book signing. The photographer was feeling creative and took a picture of it. That was the photo they used for our article. Nothing says the Ailes Brothers of Terror better than Elvis Presley. What possessed the editor of the paper to choose a picture unrelated to the article as that photo? At least, the reporter from the Post Tribune, who stopped by to do an article about the book fair, used a picture of us for the article in their newspaper.

I wrote this totally sarcastic story out of anger over the incident. I'm a big Elvis fan. I love his music. I love books about him. I own his movies on DVD. There are a lot of tidbits throughout the story that diehard Elvis fans will pick up on that non diehard fans won't realize it's a reference to him. People wish he was still alive. Hell, imagine how many more songs he would have recorded if he had lived longer.

This story is as it was truly meant to be; me making fun of myself. The people described outside my front door are my actual neighbors.

Twisted Twins: I wrote this story for Jen and Sylvia Soska, The Twisted Twins, the horror masterminds behind the movies "Dead Hooker In A Trunk", "American Mary" and "See No Evil 2". I wrote this story in the same style similar to all of their movies. I had the pleasure of meeting them a year ago at a horror convention. I've been a fan of theirs ever since. There are many references to

"American Mary" and it is as twisted as they are. They believe in having strong female characters and I didn't disappoint them. This is the most demented story I have ever written.

Marriage Zquality: After the backlash from the Republicans and the Christian Right after the Supreme Court ruling in favor of gay marriage, I wrote a zombie story based on it. People will have different opinions on what the meaning behind the story is truly about. What happens in the story parallels aspects of the holocaust and what happened to Anne Frank and her family. It's my "never forget, it can happen again" story.

Russo Jones is named after John Russo, the father of zombie movies and fiction. Thanks for making the genre popular.

In the Hollies Style: This story was written on no sleep after 2:00 am. On very little sleep, my stories become too bizarre.

I've been a huge fan of the Hollies since I heard "The Air That I Breathe" for the first time in 1994, twenty years after it had been released as a single. Over the next twenty years, I searched far and wide for every B-side and non-album track I could get my hands on. I have every song that has been released now on MP3 format. My love for the Hollies outweighs my love for every other band. The story about the Hollies is totally made up obviously; it is based on the history of the band up to when Allan Clarke first left the band right after the album "Distant Light" was released. Yes, I've made some changes to the time line since Bernie Calvert didn't officially join the band until 1966.

Elton John also makes an appearance in the story since he did the piano work for two of their songs: "He Ain't Heavy, He's My Brother" and "I Can't Tell A Bottom From the Top".

This story is complete fiction and there is no evidence that they were ever vampire slayers.

Claws Vs Mecha Cat: This is a sequel to "Claws" from "Catfurnado, Zombies and One Killer Doll". This is another story written for fans of all the offbeat horror films from the SyFy Channel and the original "Godzilla" franchise. Will there be another story? Is there a "Claws 3: Oh Hell No!" in the future? Only time will tell.

Every year my friend and I go to the Chicago Auto Show. I figured it was time to use that in one of my stories.

The shark they spotted in Lake Michigan that vanished is the shark from my story "Shark Transporter" from "Zombie Command: A Horror Anthology".

I hope that nobody saw the surprised warped ending coming. I just couldn't end the story with a happy ending.

Rastus, A Warrior's Quest & Shelana's Quest: Both of these stories are teaser stories for my upcoming fantasy novel "Beast Within". I'm pushing for a March 2016 release date. Keep checking http://www.derekailes.com for further updates. I post to my blog almost every Sunday.

I hope this journey has been thrilling and entertaining and everybody enjoyed all the stories from both mine and James Coon's minds.

I want to thank all of those who have helped or inspired me with this project:

Linda Byers & Amber Harmon for finding all of JC's stories and saving them for me.
Jeff Elkins, Bob Moulesong and everybody else at Short Fiction Break for supporting my writing career this past year.
Indiana Writers' Consortium and all of its members who have supported Mark and my writing career.
Carolyn Ailes, my mother, who has been editing these stories and helping me improve them.
Mark Cusco Ailes for being my beta reader.
John Russo for creating the first zombie masterpiece and starting the zombie revolution.
Jen & Sylvia Soska for proving to the world that women can dominate the horror industry, and we shouldn't view women as the victims in the horror genre.
James Coon: for sharing these stories and adventures with me. I will always cherish our fifteen years of friendship.

Thank you for reading Musings From A Demented Mind. Whether you liked it or not, I hope you'll take a moment to leave a review on Amazon. Reviews are vitally important to me as an author both to help me market my book and to improve my writing in the future. Thank you!

Made in the USA
Charleston, SC
23 September 2015